Contrary to Popular Belief

Neil Anthes

Clink
Street

London | New York

STORY TIMELINE

44	B.C.E.	The assassination of Julius Caesar
29	B.C.E.	Octavius gains control of the Empire
27	B.C.E.	Roman Senate confers title of Augustus
14	A.D.	Death of Augustus
14–37	A.D.	The reign of Tiberius
37–41	A.D.	The reign of Caligula
41–54	A.D.	The reign of Claudius
51	A.D.	Death of Jeshua Christus
325	A.D.	The Council of Nicaea
1945	A.D.	The Nag Hammadi discovery

ROME
5 A.D.

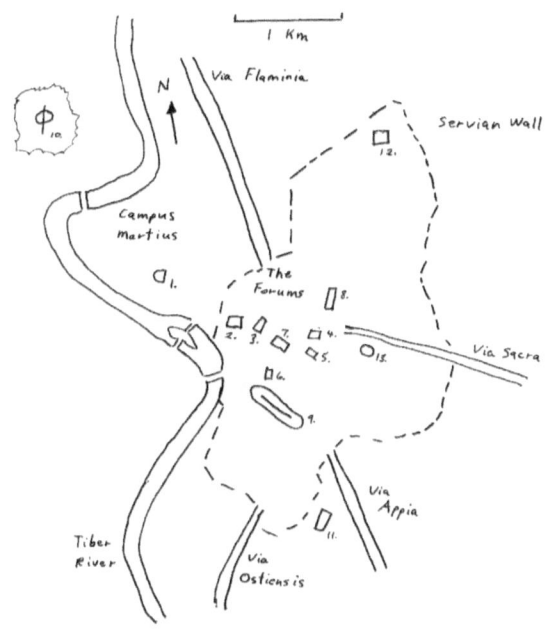

1. Pompey Theater
2. Temple of Jupiter
3. Temple of Saturn
4. Divus Julius
   (Temple of Julius Caesar)
5. Temple of Vesta
6. Temple of Cybele

07. Basilica Julia
08. Senate
09. Circus Maximus
10. Vaticanum
11. Baths
12. Baths
13. Future Flavian Amphitheater

ROME
MARCH 15, 44 B.C.E.

Beneath the blood-splattered statue of his old rival and friend Pompey, the defeated body of Julius Caesar lies lifeless on the floor of the Pompey Theater. The wounds from twenty-three dagger blows have taken the last breath of life from the leader of Republican Rome. His stained and torn toga is pulled over his head in a display of self-honor. He would not allow his attackers to see his face enter death.

Jupiter, the supreme God, summons the Goddess Venus, protector of the Julius family. She is instructed to rescue the spirit from the corpse and carry it to the high celestial heavens. She is then directed to transform that soul into a star that will forever shine above the Forum and the city of Rome.

As word spreads that the very popular "Dictator for Life" Julius Caesar has been assassinated, riots break out around the Campus Martius where the theater is located. Soon the rioters cross the city walls searching for the leaders of the murder plot.

In an attempt to maintain civil peace, Marcus Aemilius Lepidus, an ally of Caesar, summons his soldiers to the Campus Martius. To ensure calm among the people, he declares that revenge of Caesar's death will be achieved by immediately killing those involved. Marcus Antonius, another close friend of the fallen Caesar, persuades Lepidus to restrain his soldiers from attacking the perpetrators. The two allies agree to address the Senate the next day to seek a compromise or an understanding with the conspirators.

The crowds soon learn the names of the leaders of this treacherous treason, Gaius Cassius Longinus and his brother-in-law, the self-absorbed Marcus Junius Brutus. As the crowds swell and become hostile, the two men retreat to the Temple of Jupiter for protection. Brutus addresses the mob and tries to calm them with reason. "Caesar had become very arrogant. He was not satisfied with his birthday being declared a public holiday nor his birth month, Quinctilus, being renamed July in his honor. It is rumoured he was about to change his title of Dictator for Life of the Roman Republic to King Caesar. This could not to be allowed. Jupiter is the King of Rome."

~

The elite of Rome knew the history of Caesar's activities. After consolidating his power by eliminating his two co-councils, he had unilaterally reformed the Senate. These changes angered the traditionalists. However, his land and tax reforms made him very popular with low and middle class Romans. His formation of a police force for Rome, which made the city much safer, also enhanced his popularity with the masses. Reforms rumoured to be established in the future included abolishing the Senate completely. Whether true or false, this led to his demise at the hands of traditional Republicans.

However, the common people outnumbered the elite. The body of Caesar was retrieved from the Pompey Theater by the crowd and carried through the streets of Rome to his home. They wanted to have the funeral ritual performed at the Forum. On March 20, as the traditionalists were preparing the funeral pyre on the

Campus Martius, the commoners removed the reclaimed corpse from the official proceedings by force and took it to the Forum where it was cremated. The ashes were then taken to the family mausoleum on the Campus Martius. Thus, the leader of Rome was buried by his subjects, not the elite.

The angry mob then turned against Cassius and Brutus. They swarmed the villas of the two men and attempted to burn down their homes. Disguised as slaves, the two immediately fled Rome towards the Eastern province of Macedonia.

A few days later the high Priestess of Vesta revealed Caesar's will. His declared heir would not be his son by the Egyptian Queen Cleopatra VII but Gaius Octavius, a distant blood relative, his adopted son. Octavius immediately began to arrange the funeral games to be held four months later to honor his father. He also formed a governing triumvirate with Caesar's close friends Lepidus and Marcus Antonius. All were committed to avenging the death of their leader and comrade.

Soon the transformed spirit of Caesar would streak across the sky as a long-haired star, brighter than the sun. The illumination would show all of Rome and her conquered lands that Caesar had been accepted into the realm of the gods and lived among them as one himself.

The participants at the funeral games were awe-struck at the transformation of their fallen leader. He had become a celestial god shining above Rome. Every day for seven days during the games, the star of Caesar appeared during the eleventh hour of daylight. Octavius explained to all that the deification of his father by Jupiter and Venus must be recognized by himself and all the Senate.

Octavius started the campaign to honor his father and avenge his death under this brilliant heavenly body, a show of the will of the gods. The immensely popular Julius

Caesar, now a god, would help ensure success for his heir.

All now acknowledged Octavius as the chosen divine Son to deliver Rome into her deserving glory. It would take more than one military victory over the leaders of the assassins, help from his co-rulers (whom he would eventually have to dispose of) and a proclamation by the Senate, but this Divi Filius would eventually usher in many years of relative peaceful existence for Rome.

All declared that the "long-haired star" symbolized the birth of the rule of Rome by Octavius, the first Emperor of the new Roman Empire. It was a decree of the gods, a divine intention. All must acknowledge this sacred event. The gods must be worshipped, appeased and obeyed.

CHANG'AN, CHINA
SUMMER 44 B.C.E.

The Chang'an traders of jade, tea, porcelain vases, bronze ornaments, and especially colorful silk, are preparing their camels, horses and carts for the first leg of the long trip to Rome. All the supplies for shipping are procured at this Chinese city. It is humming with frantic activity. For the merchants who choose the northern land route to the west, all goods start their passage here in the capital city. Everything must be securely prepared, as there will be many transfers along the way. Items will be traded at each stop at the oasis towns. Not all goods will reach Rome, but those that do will command a high price and will be purchased only by the upper class. Strands of bright silk sewn onto togas are a popular sign of wealth.

Few men have actually completed the entire journey, as it requires many months away from productive activity. Some workers will travel to a few stopovers on the way if they need the work. The goods will change hands physically many times, creating wealth for the towns along the way.

The Chinese merchants' wares are sought by all in the west. For many years they have accepted glassware and golden embroidery in exchange. Fine woven carpets are also popular, as well as gold, silver, ivory and dazzling precious gems. Saffron, figs and grape seeds have introduced the Chinese to Western foods as well as wines made from fruit rather than rice.

Suddenly, late in the day there is a brilliant broom star streaking across the sky. Some workers stop to observe the phenomenon. Older people say they have seen similar happenings before. They will consult the astronomers for any significance. These men have recorded the different shapes of these dazzling celestial visitors for centuries. While the tails always point away from the sun, the heads of the stars and the shapes of the tail can vary immensely. Over two dozen different patterns have been recorded over the past several hundred years. This specific broom star probably has made visits many years ago, more than once. It is believed these stars are a sign for the direction of the country or its leaders. Perhaps the Emperor has ruled badly lately. Perhaps the karma of the country will be tested.

Whatever the significance, the merchants return to their tasks. There is no time to waste. The first group of animals and carts going overland will be leaving at the first light of day. There have been more attacks by thieves on the trade route lately, so for safety, the caravan will be larger and a more remote road will be taken.

Perhaps the unusual star is an omen for a good season of trading. China may reap rich rewards from the fruits of her labor.

ROME
TEMPLE TO CYBELE
SEPTEMBER 44 B.C.E.

Atia prays nervously in front of the shrine for Magna Mater—the Great Mother—at the Circus Maximus. She offers wine and sacred bread that was baked on the hearth of the divine fire in the Temple of Vesta. Vesta is the Goddess of the Hearth for all of Rome. Her Vestal Virgins attend to the hallowed flame, never allowing it to be extinguished. They provide immortal bread and cakes for offerings to the Deities. They also maintain all records of the houses of Rome. A man's recorded death will is overseen at the Temple of Vesta.

Atia is gripped with apprehension and fear for the safety of her son; her house and home may be threatened. She knows her offerings must be greater today than mere nourishment and sustenance for the Goddess. Her son's life may be in grave peril. The Magna Mater's protection must be summoned beyond question. Atia must be sure the Goddess hears her desperate request.

She can see the Temple to the Great Mother, Cybele, in the distance on Palatine hill. She climbs the long stone steps to the entrance. She enters and approaches the Priest. With a worried voice she says, "I am Atia Balba Caesonia, the niece of Julius Caesar and the mother of

Gaius Octavius, the heir designated by the assassinated Dictator for Life. My son is now known as Gaius Julius Caesar Octavianus. I know there are still many Republicans who oppose the ideas of Caesar and believe my son will continue the policies of the Dictator. I fear for his life now that he carries Caesar's name. Also, he will be required to do battle with the assassins. He is young and inexperienced in armed conflicts. He needs deific protection. I must offer my sacrifice to the Great Mother today."

The Priest agrees. The ritual is commenced. The mother of Octavius is prepared to offer her sacrifice. She is washed and cleansed then placed in the lower level compartment beneath the floor in front of the altar. Through the many holes in the floor she can see the shafts of bright golden sunlight bouncing off the bright marble walls of the enclosure. A great bull is adorned with green and golden garlands and chained to the posts before the altar above her. The priest sharpens the ceremonial dagger. With agile speed and accuracy, the neck of the magnificent beast is sliced on both sides. The gushing warm blood showers Atia and covers her completely. She feels a wondrous release from her fears. The beast falls to its knees. The ritual has commenced.

The entrails of lungs, gall bladder, liver and heart are gathered and placed in a large iron pot. The blood is collected and also added to the pot. Wine, flour and salt are added as the mixture cooks. It is then placed on the sacred flame to be incinerated to ash and released for Cybele's enjoyment. The meat of the sacrificed beast is roasted, filling the temple with a tasty aroma. It will be offered to all as word is spread throughout the Forum that food is available at the temple. Cybele will protect, even in death. She will resurrect Octavius should he be taken in battle. That is the power of Cybele, protector of Rome for over one hundred and fifty years.

The Magna Mater or Goddess Cybele arrived from Greece to protect Rome from the threatening military attacks of Hannibal. Cybele herself had caused the death of her lover by her jealousy. In her grief, she petitioned Zeus to bring him back to life. When the spring sun brought life back to the vegetation of the earth, her request was granted. Her lover was resurrected, ascended back to the heavens, and spared an afterlife of suffering. He now lives for eternity with her and the gods. All of Rome knows that when Cybele is appeased, she too will resurrect the chosen loved one if death grabs him from their embrace. His spirit will not be condemned to live underground in the earth as all ancestors do, but will soar to the celestial heavens and enjoy eternal happiness.

Atia leaves with a peaceful heart. She knows the danger that lies ahead for Octavius, both in Rome and the provinces. She will pray to Cybele whenever she passes one of the many shrines erected in her honor throughout Rome. Cybele is the mother protector and deliverer of resurrection for eternal life.

EASTERN ROMAN
PROVINCES
42 B.C.E.

Several legions of soldiers were hired by Octavianus and Marcus Antonius. They were charged with hunting down Caesar's assassins and avenging his death. Lepidus was elected to oversee the stability of Rome until the traitors were destroyed. Some of his legions were donated to the campaign. After two years of preparation, the hunt for the traitors commenced. The massive assembly of fighters headed east.

The despised leaders of the tyrants were finally located near Philippi in Macedonia, near northern Greece. Their armies were assembled in two camps on high ground overlooking a marshy plain with mountains on two sides. The avengers planned an attack to separate the camps, a strategy that would weaken the enemies' forces.

With over one hundred thousand men on both sides, a horrific battle raged between the armies of Octavianus and Brutus. The armies of Marcus Antonius and the armies of Cassius fought for the second hill.

Marcus Antonius had fast success over Cassius as he was able to draw the enemy into battle on the marshy plain below the hill and then attack their camp on the high ground. When the combatants for Cassius saw the destruction of their camp, they retreated. Cassius, however, found refuge with a small number of his legionaries. When it became apparent that he would be captured by Marcus Antonius, he committed suicide.

Meanwhile, Brutus had success against the legions of Octavianus, a much younger and less experienced military commander than Antonius. However, Octavianus was ill and hid in the marshes, thus avoiding capture by Brutus.

Upon regrouping the legions of both Octavianus and Marcus Antonius, the combined forces were able to divide the fighters for Brutus. Octavianus attacked the camp while Antonius pursued Brutus into the mountains. When the legions fighting for Brutus pleaded for clemency from Marcus Antonius, Marcus Junius Brutus took his own life.

Marcus Antonius had demonstrated his experience and superiority in battle over the young Octavianus. Both claimed victory. However, being the heir designated by Julius Caesar, only Octavianus would celebrate victory in Rome. He would later prove a master at politics and nurturing loyalty as he clashed with his co-leaders. He would eventually become the sole Emperor of Rome.

Marcus Antonius remained in the Eastern provinces and attempted to revive the plans of conquest for Rome envisioned by Caesar before he was murdered. He would eventually petition the Egyptian Queen Cleopatra VII for help in the campaign. He would get distracted and abandon his plans.

Octavianus retuned to Rome. His armies gathered about the Campus Martius, the field dedicated to the God of War, Mars. An altar was prepared and all celebrated before it. They gave thanks to Mars for the victory. The High Priestess of Vesta lit the sacred flame by concentrating the sun's rays onto the prepared wood. With the sacred flame glowing, burnt offerings of cinnamon, red clover and meat were made to Mars. Mars was pleased. All of Rome gave prayers of thanks to the gods and the soldiers. Octavianus was revered and cheered by all. He had defeated the destroyers. The sacrifice of protection to Cybele for Octavianus had been successful.

Then Octavianus boarded his chariot and his soldiers put down their weapons. They paraded down Via Flaminia, through the gate to the Forum and proceeded to the Temple of Jupiter. In front of an enthusiastic crowd, Octavianus offered his victories to this supreme god. Offerings of wine and sacred bread, baked by the Vestal Virgins, were also given. This long-standing custom and ritual had always been performed by victorious generals upon their return to Rome.

ROME
29 B.C.E.

Octavianus, as Caesar's designated heir to power, realized he needed to remove his co-rulers. Marcus Antonius had abandoned Rome for Cleopatra but his ambitions were still a threat. He prepared for battle. This time it was at sea. The clash took place off the southwest coast of Greece in the Ionian Sea. His shrewd general Agrippa defeated the combined navies of Cleopatra and Marcus Antonius. With defeat looming, both Cleopatra and Marcus Antonius abandoned their troops and fled to Egypt. The two then committed suicide.

Lepidus some years earlier had been displaced over the Sicily campaign when his legions defected to Octavianus. However, he was allowed to retain his Senate seat but remained powerless. In retaliation, his son attempted an assassination of Octavianus. When the plot was discovered, he was killed. Lepidus was spared and allowed to live in exiled obscurity in Italy until his death. Octavianus was now the sole ruler of Rome.

As sole commander, Octavianus' first task was to ensure all saw him as a son of a god. His rule must be viewed as divinely ordered; it was the will of the gods. His reign was born under the brilliant star of Caesar during the funeral games.

Julius Caesar, now resident among the gods and the first Roman to be embraced by all the celestial Deities, must be honored. His temple, which was approved by the Senate in 42 B.C.E., would be dedicated by Octavianus. The statue of Caesar with the star across his forehead was placed where all could view it whether inside or outside the Divus Julius temple. The wildly popular Julius Caesar was now immortalized and had a place among all of Rome and would protect all of her subjects.

The Cult of Caesar was initiated to promote the worship of Caesar as a god. As sons of a god, the current Emperor and his successors were to be considered divine and worshipped accordingly. For Rome to rise to her glory, emperors must be revered and glorified.

Octavianus needed to change his name. The name Octavianus was associated with battle, blood and revenge. To maintain his grip on power, it had been necessary to dispose of his challengers and their heirs. Now however, the Emperor and a son of the God Caesar, his name must reflect his divinity. In 27 B.C.E., the senate bestowed upon Octavianus the name Imperator Caesar Divi Filius Augustus. Imperator, the name troops give their leader after successful battles; Caesar, the name of his father; Divi Filius, Son of God; and Augustus, the illustrious one. Now calling himself Augustus, he immediately started to erect statues of himself in temples. They were placed beside the god each temple was built to honor. Augustus must be seen by all as equal to the gods. The cult must flourish. It was divinely ordained by the star of Caesar, created by the supreme God Jupiter and Goddess Venus.

The first statues were placed in the Eastern provinces, as their history of granting deity status to mortal rulers would make the concept more acceptable. They had deified Alexander the Great after his military conquests. Egyptian gods had been personified through their rulers for many years. Cleopatra was divine in her rule, which made her extremely attractive to both Julius Caesar and

Marcus Antonius. They had both desired sacred status for their offspring to strengthen their hold on power in Rome. Ironically, Octavianus had to ensure the murder of her offspring by both Caesar and Antonius to protect his own power.

Eventually, the temples of Rome also would see statues of Augustus among the statues of their gods. The cult must flourish. The Emperor must be seen as divine and an equal to the gods to maintain his power. The future of Rome depended upon Imperial worship.

THE LAKE OF GALILEE
WINTER SOLSTICE 7 A.D.

High atop the rocky cliffs overlooking the large lake to the west, the young priestess watches the evening sun drown in the water. It is defeated and death consumes it. Sitting still, with eyes closed and hands held high, she beckons Helios to guide the sun through the underworld and bring Sol back to the east in the morning, bringing warmth to the lands and supporting life on the earth for all—plant, animal or mortal.

The Sun is the supreme fire power of nature, the Supreme Deity of the natural world. Nothing is more fretful and threatening than witnessing its death every evening. It appears to transform itself into a Divine Ghost. It will wander through the underworld tonight before rising in the east tomorrow.

The priestess trusts that the God Sun will return for another day to bring its life-giving warmth to the earth. Tomorrow, as every day, it will evolve three times. Firstly, after his predicted morning arrival in the east, he is the Father of the Dawn. He travels to the high noon sky where he is transformed to become the son of the early morning Father God. The Son of the God Sun provides maximum warmth and light, offering hope and health to all mortals and living things. Then, fading and aging at day's end, Sol retreats to become his own Holy Ghost, travelling the underworld once again.

Throughout the dark hours, the young priestess remains in her seated position. The chill of the longest night nips at her face. Eventually she can detect the faint light rays of the resurrected and reborn Sun in the east. Her heart races with anticipation of the celebration of the return of the supreme Father God.

A small altar is prepared. The priestess arranges cedar and juniper boughs and lights a bonfire by concentrating the first burst of the Sun's rays onto some wood fragments. Clutching a small stick of wood, she scratches a symbol into the ground in front of the fire. It is two lines intersecting equally, with the second divided into two unequal lengths—a cross. This image represents the travels of the Sun God through the celestial heavens over the year.

The priestess repeats the words she has been taught by her grandmothers ... "With joy and thanksgiving, we hail the return of the divine and supreme Sun, rescued from its own death, as it now begins its cycle again to the long warm days." The priestess walks around the four points of the cross. Starting at the equal side ... "Oh Easterly Heavens, we welcome and revere the new beginning that awaits." She continues to the longest point ... "Oh Southern Heavens, we honor your full days and continued warmth; we thank you for providing the coming harvest." She proceeds to the other side of the equal line ... "The coming days will shorten, we will sacrifice some of your givings back to you, oh Celestial Being, to ensure your safe journey." She now reaches the top of the cross, the shortest line from the center intersection, and chants ... "Oh hallowed God of Light, we welcome your return, we honor your way as you light our path. Your heat and light will raise all things from the dead. Life will be restored to every man who sees you. You will feed the multitudes with your light. You are the Supreme Spirit. Your journey to full expression awaits."

The young priestess then sits and faces the eastern horizon. She crosses her legs and closes her eyes. She feels the increasing warmth of the rising sun on her cool skin. She knows her life will be good again. She is renewed. Joy swells within her soul. She worships the almighty Sun and all his glorious phases throughout the day and the year.

A small contingent of scholarly travellers headed to Damascus see a faraway flame atop the eastern cliffs of the Lake of Galilee. Basking in the warm morning sun, they continue their journey along the eastern road of the lake without investigation. The fire to the west disappears.

A young boy in Palestine dashes to the shoreline and gazes out over the Mediterranean Sea; he also welcomes the rays of light as they frolic upon the gently moving waters. They chase away the longest night of the year. He admires the sea birds gliding across the horizon. He witnesses the gentle rolling of the waves kissing the stones and sand of the shore. He observes the moon and the stars fading from the night sky. He marvels at the wonders of creation. He senses his soul. He feels his innate connection with all of creation and intuitively knows that he is part of this magnificence. Awe and wonderment fill his being. He feels the sacred flame within his heart. His spirit feels free. He communes with his inner sun, his inward lighted spirit. He knows his personal sun acts just like the natural sun. His inner spirit gives life to all his body and its functions and its emanations, just as the worldly sun gives life to all the earth and its manifestations.

A heavy feeling descends upon him. The next Passover festival is approaching. He is not inspired by the required attendance and observance of rituals at the Temple of Jerusalem. These customs do not bring him closer to his divinity. To him, they are stifling and self-destructive. He intensely dislikes the mandatory treks to Jerusalem. The crowds are enormous. The word of God as told by the Pharisees requires every man, woman and child to attend the Temple in Jerusalem for Passover. Caravans of people travel from places afar, even Rome. The hundreds and thousands of people who descend upon the city make for an arduous time. It is not what his soul longs for. He is drawn to the wonder of the sea, the sky and all the creatures that inhabit the earth. That is his Temple.

Jeshua knows he cannot put up with false truths for much longer. However, he is just a boy. He must follow the traditions demanded of his ancestors and his family. He must remain silent and not question the Temple priests, nor the Pharisees, guardians of the oral traditions of his culture as set out by the laws of Moses. He must also obey the elders of his village. He pushes the blissful thought of his personal natural Temple from his mind. Breathing in the cool morning air, he drinks in one long last look at the wonderful sea, his heart filled with joy, then turns his back to his divine friends and runs, half dancing, back to his village.

JERUSALEM
SPRING 9 A.D.

The long journey from his village to Jerusalem for the Passover celebrations is making Jeshua tired and dusty. The days are getting longer now, so they can travel farther each day. The full moon brightens the night sky. Being the first born, he must gather with the others of his stature the day before the festivities begin and fast in remembrance of God's protection. The one-day fast is a sign of gratitude to God for sparing the Jewish firstborns when he destroyed the firstborn children of Egyptian families for disobeying his commands. The spectacle of rituals in his culture is entertaining to Jeshua, yet he sees the folly in them. Each year, the Temple priests change when the fast should end, before sunset or after. To him, this shows that religious customs are contrived by man, not divinely ordained. The sun always arrives to its position in the sky exactly on time each season, as preordained by divine Nature. To Jeshua, that which is created by natural divine intelligence is the real law. For now, he does not criticize, as he would be considered an apostate and be excluded from the festive meals. If he broke with tradition, his family would be extremely upset. His Truth is smothered today.

The sound of hundreds of bleating lambs and goats waiting for the ceremonial slaughter is annoying Jeshua and the others. The time for these animals will soon be here and the noise will cease. Jeshua is often placed in charge of the family's lamb while en route to Jerusalem. He enjoys the responsibility. He also hands the coins to the toll collectors along the roads and upon entering the city. These taxmen are not welcomed in the community, even during Passover; they are considered corrupt agents of Rome.

As dusk approaches, the doors of the Temple are closed. All inside have paid the mandatory half-shekel to the Temple's treasury. They stand shoulder to shoulder; no space between any man, woman or child. The law states they must be inside the Temple walls to be properly blessed by Jehovah when the festivities begin. However, since the Temple cannot hold the hundreds of thousands who have travelled to Jerusalem, the High Priest has expanded the boundary that is considered holy during Passover. If a group travelling from Rome or other far-away places is not within that boundary at the allotted time, a second Passover will be performed the next month. Until that time, they must wait in Jerusalem and cannot return to their homes. A representative of all groups within the expanded boundary must bring a ceremonial lamb to the Temple for slaughter. The trumpets blare to announce the beginning of the celebration and the choir sings. All present join in song as do those outside the walls. The divinely ordered night festival begins.

The first ritual of the feast is the ceremonial slaughter of the goats and lambs. Timing of the sacrifices is very specific, laid down by divine law as interpreted by the Pharisees and Temple governors. The priests work at lightning speed. The blood is gathered in gold and silver vessels then poured onto the altar. The animals are taken to the many roasting ovens spread throughout Jerusalem and roasted whole, one animal per family or group. It is dictated again by God that the ritual meal must be taken with community, not alone. Everyone, rich or poor, partakes of the festival. All the meat must be consumed before sunrise and no bones may be broken. That which is left uneaten must be burned.

The same sacred service is performed by each group. They remember their forefathers' suffering in Egypt and the plagues sent by God to punish the Pharaoh and his nation. They recall God's hand in their miraculous escape through the Sea of Reeds and the subsequent destruction of the pursuing Egyptian armies behind them. They recall the divine laws for how they should conduct their lives laid down by God as revealed through Moses. They declare the Passover holy, a dictate from God. The first of four mandatory glasses of ceremonial wine is poured. Wine is a symbol of the joy experienced by their forefathers when they were released from slavery. The four glasses represent the four great merits shown by the children of Israel while in exile and servitude: they did not change their Hebrew names, they continued to speak their language, they remained highly moral towards their captors, and they remained loyal to one another. All the bread and food eaten during this festive gathering is symbolic of the history of the Jewish people. Upon completion of the ritual meal that honors the past, the doors are opened. This symbolically invites the future Messiah of the people, as described by the prophet Elijah, to enter into the lives of the Jewish people. This Messiah will restore Hebrew rule and law to the lands. When the fourth glass is finished, the Almighty is again recognized for his unique guidance of the Jewish people and is honored as the creator of the entire Universe. His continued protection for the people is implored.

After seven days of festivities and remembrance of the heritage and history of their people, the Passover is finished. Jeshua with his family and the other villagers leave Jerusalem for the journey back to their homes.

He cannot find the spiritual depth with his people in Jerusalem that he feels when standing by the seashore. The housing and feeding of thousands of people is daunting for him. Individual spirituality is the farthest thing from the gathering. Even the fasting in gratitude to God for saving the firstborns while in slavery in Egypt does not give him a sense of centeredness with his Creator and inner sun. He wishes he could share his understanding of life, but he knows the elders demand adherence to tradition. Anything else would be heresy and he would be banned from his culture. He would be denied participation in future Passovers.

He longs to share the passion he feels when he is by the sea and in the wilderness. It is there he experiences the real God of Life, not in the Temple of Jerusalem. His heartache grows with each passing year. He knows that someday he must be true to himself and his Creator. For now, he will enjoy his boyhood for a few more years.

The dusty road is making him thirsty.

THE SACRED CIRCLE
15 A.D.

Jeshua always enjoys his journey to the scared circle at night. He pauses in the cool air often to gaze up in wonder at the sparkling stars and moon in the darkened heavens. He feels so close to Creation during these sojourns through the wilderness. He finds peace and inner joy while in contact with Nature. Resting against a smooth rock while marvelling at the stars winking at him from their celestial playgrounds, he is lulled into a light sleep.

An Angel in long colorful robes floats towards him. Brilliant white light radiates all around her, accentuating her stunning beauty. She smiles and gazes into his eyes. Her eyes are like windows of a kaleidoscope of color and joy. They shine with a brilliance of ten thousand suns, yet do not harm his eyes. He is bathed in immense joy and love beyond anything he has felt on earth. She speaks softly to him, saying he will be an instrument of Truth. His time will come after his apprenticeship with spirit. He will be a bridge between two realities, an instrument of spreading understanding and compassion. She says to him, "Be not afraid of the Pharisees, for they are the uninformed. They need to shed themselves of the ignorance which is their choice."

The Angel is accompanied by several smaller deities, all surrounded by brilliant white pulsating light and playing flutes or humming like bees in their hives. The combination of pure joy, bliss, harmonious sound and unsurpassed beauty assures Jeshua of his divine soul. He envisions himself in the future speaking to many congregations of people throughout Palestine. The times seem different. Then the Angel fades away, smiling directly into his heart. He awakes to the awesome magnificence of the dark night sky. A silvery shooting star races across the horizon. He feels indescribable joy.

Jeshua stands up and locates the Star of Saturn far off in the dark purple heavens. As expected, it is at his feet, indicating it is time, a time for new directions in his life. After the last Passover, he had tried to discuss his knowledge of the Truth of life with the Pharisees but they would not listen with an open mind. He knows his time here is finished and his life must pursue a different course. The alignment with the Star of Saturn now confirms his sense of purpose. The heavenly Angel has spoken the truth. A new door is about to open, a new pathway is to be revealed.

Jeshua can see the faint glowing rays of sunlight to the east. He says good-bye to this holy place and returns to the village.

THE ROAD HOME

Stopping at the seashore, Jeshua watches the sea birds gracefully glide over the waves, their wingtips just touching the water. The morning sun bounces off the crests of the small waves, saying good morning to all who observe. This is his Temple, being by the sea. The sails of the trade ships leaving the port of Gaza in southern Palestine can be seen on the distant horizon. They carry spices, cloves, black pepper, medicines, jewels and silk that have been transported by camel caravans up the Arabian Peninsula from India and China. The goods are then shipped by sea to other ports on the Mediterranean, mainly Alexandria in Egypt and Ostia, the seaport at the mouth of the Tiber River servicing Rome. The harvest of frankincense from the Boswellia trees of Arabia and Africa as well as myrrh are also transported through Gaza to Alexandria and Rome. They are used as incense to cover the many odours that thrive in large populated areas, and as flavoring for wine. They are also used as perfumes and medicines and during embalming rituals in Egypt. These dried tree saps and resins have made many people along the trade routes wealthy.

The many camel and horse caravans and the way stations along the spice and incense routes that cross the Peninsula could use a person of his talents. He is trained in the use of wood for construction and repair. He considers seeking employment at one of the many oases that provide rest and shelter to the traders and travellers. Each section of the route has its regular work force. They transfer goods from the incoming caravan to those who will carry them to the next station. Repairs are done at each mustering location.

He has heard that the city of Palmyra in Syria has been growing rapidly as a result of the wealth from trading in goods. Traders are arriving from both the sea spice routes from India and land trade routes from China. Jeshua knows some of his Jewish brethren have moved there to take advantage of employment opportunities at the expanded facilities. Even though it is in foreign Arab land, the few Jewish people brave enough to venture there have been accepted without harshness. Some are also acting as agents for the traders.

Jeshua knows in his heart it is now time to leave his village. He decides to venture north to Palmyra. He will miss the sea; however, his awe of Creation will be reinforced within the realm of the wilderness. Living at one of the largest palm oases in Syria will be enriching. Being a fully qualified carpenter who can also work with stone, he has the skills to support himself.

He arrives home resolved to follow through on his plans. He bids farewell to his parents, his brother James and all the villagers, assuring them he will return in seven years.

His spirit feels free, more alive than ever, and certainly much lighter than he has ever felt in the Temple of Jerusalem. He will not miss the visits there. Though he respects his traditions, he knows he can no longer honor them. Saturn has his lessons to teach. A celestial Angel will be looking over him.

A VILLA IN ROME
16 A.D.

The magistrate kneels before the small lararium built of marble and embedded into the stone wall beside the entrance way. With his toga pulled over his head, he kisses his right hand and touches the cool marble. He pours some wine into the small round stone bowl beside the warm sacred flame. Then, pouring more wine onto the ground beside the lararium, he blesses it as it disappears into the soil. He drinks the rest.

Placing his right hand over his heart, he prays, "Be ye well, divine Lares Familius, you always preserve and maintain our house and household."

He places a small piece of sacred cake baked by the Vestal Virgins into the stone bowl. Then he eats the rest of the offering. The wine and the cake will be nourishment for his deceased ancestors who continually watch over and protect his home and family. They must be thanked for watching over them during the night. He eats the cake and drinks the wine in their memory. The ancestors must be acknowledged every day to ensure their continued protection.

A dash of saffron is placed on the sacred flame beside the small stone bowl. It is reduced to ash. As in all burnt offerings, the fire releases the spirit of the material being consumed. The spirit of the herb is now able to favor the supreme god Jupiter who will, when appeased by this offering, grant abundance to his home and household, family and slaves alike.

He stretches his hands outwards and upward towards the celestial god and prays, "Jupiter, I offer this spirit to you with good prayers so that you may be propitious to me, my children, my house and my household."

He whispers a prayer of thanks to the deceased who live underground and again to the celestial God Jupiter, his choice of gods for this day. Tomorrow he will appease Vesta, guardian of the sacred flame of Rome, as his family will be receiving visitors to their home during the festival. Her preference will be a small portion of lamb, consumed to ash by the flame she protects.

His daily morning rituals complete, he uncovers his head and briskly walks down the darkened cobbled streets of Rome to the Temple of Saturn. The shortest day of the year is four days away; there is little sunlight this time of year. His evening offerings at the lararium on his return will be done by candlelight. He hopes Jupiter will be gracious. The ancestors will understand. They remember the festivals. He hopes he poured enough wine into the ground for the deceased to enjoy, as it is the beginning of a long celebration.

ROME
SATURN'S TEMPLE
DECEMBRIS 17, 16 A.D.

As a recently appointed magistrate to the Roman court, Lupus Antonius Brutus is well aware of his family name and its links to Roman history. His ancient ancestor, Lucius Junius Brutus, was one of the founders of the Republic Rome. In his own way, one of the assassins of Julius Caesar, Marcus Junius Brutus, was a co-founder of the Roman Empire that eventually grew from the disposal of Caesar. Lupus Antonius Brutus has no desire to influence Roman history. His life is completely self-serving. He has come to the temple to revel in the festivities.

The shrieking of piglets bouncing off the stark grey granite columns can be heard from the first stone step leading up to the temple. Once sacrificed, which cannot be soon enough for Brutus, the fresh meat will be roasted over the hot orange embers of the glowing fire pit.

Brutus enjoys the variety of cooking aromas emanating from the fire pit as well as the laughter and noise of Saturn's Temple this time of year. The hollow statue of Saturn is filled with olive oil. Decorations are placed among the tall stone columns. The decorations, mainly green laurel bows and gold and yellow candles, are symbols of the celebration of Saturnalia. Green represents the abundance of a successful harvest. Gold is the color of the life-giving sun that gives the light and warmth upon which the harvest depends. Many of the objects are round or circular, honoring the shape of the fiery sun.

Legend describes the god Saturn as an ancient king who showed early peoples how to plough fields and build homes. He was a good king and all prospered under his rule. When he died, it was fitting to declare him a god, build a temple in his honor and thank him with sacrifices. The temple is the oldest in the Forum, almost five hundred years old. This is Rome's oldest celebration, a festival of abundance and liberation. At least, this is how Brutus believes the festival originated.

He ponders further. Perhaps it was an Emperor or ancient king who decided Rome needed a new and different state religion. Why not import one from Syria? Or was it Persia or Babylon? Brutus wasn't sure. He recalled a Syrian festival called Sol Invicti, or "birthday of the unconquered sun". It was the celebration of the time when the winter sun stays low and still in the sky for three days and then reverses direction—just as it was now situated over the sky of Rome. The sun overcomes its own apparent appointment with death. The new light and coming warmth are anticipated and celebrated by all. He had seen the silver coins that had been pressed by Marcus Antonius shortly after Caesar's death that seemed to honor this religion. The head of the Sun God Sol was minted with the likeness of Marcus Antonius. Some of the coins were stored in the massive vault below this temple. The Treasury had been here for many centuries. Why not have the God of Prosperity watching over all the wealth of Rome?

Perhaps it was just a dream he had one night after too much wine. Brutus mumbles to himself, "It does not matter the history or significance anymore. It is a festival when all of Rome is immersed in merriment and celebration. Every subject forgets his cares and concerns for seven days."

He looks at the new statue of Emperor Augustus alongside the god Saturn. It seems an accurate portrayal of the recently deceased. The worship of the Emperor alongside the gods has been an official Imperial direction for over forty years now. Augustus' widow Livia, now called Julia Augusta, has been dedicated to entrenching this change into Roman beliefs. Emperor worship is spreading as more statues of Augustus are being erected at temples throughout the Empire. Gods who influence Roman life must be worshiped by all and the Emperor's rule must been seen as equal with the gods. However, this does not concern Brutus. He is content with his life; he feels little need to appease all the gods, just a few from time to time. He does not need the rising Cult of Emperor worship. He exercises his own power in his court.

Brutus smiles at his slaves who have ventured to Saturn's Temple, the only time of the year when they are excused from all duties. They are waiting for the games to begin. He finds the role reversal trivial but amusing; however, he is ready to fulfill his part of the tradition. Roast pig, pickled fish, figs, olives, prunes, and nuts are served to the slaves. He is the serf for the day. They laugh heartily at his required colorful clothes, a stark contrast to the formal toga he usually wears.

Brutus is easily entertained by his servants. They seem to mock him, trying to dominate him. Accustomed to being suppressed, they lack the skill to dominate others. Their feeble attempts make him laugh. Wine is poured for everyone, to excess.

Brutus recalls his visit to the newly-declared Emperor's seaside villa shortly after the death of Emperor Augustus. It is located high above a cliff and inaccessible by sea. It is guarded by the best legions. The opulence and number of slaves had been beyond his imagination. To ensure all were aware of his sinister power, Emperor Tiberius would have young boys swim under him in his pool. He demanded they gently bite his naked body as they swam past him, as if they were fish in the sea. His favorite area of attention was his manhood. If a boy refused or didn't bite in the best of ways, the Emperor would go into a rage, yank him out of the pool and throw the small victim over the cliff. The laughs of the Emperor did not cover their screams as they plummeted to the rocks below. The occasional guest who displeased the Emperor also met the same fate. The body pieces, swept out to sea, were quickly forgotten. With no proper burial in the ground, the spirit of the deceased would be tormented for eternity for disobeying the Emperor.

Brutus admires the Emperor's ability to dominate subjects both in his palaces and throughout his Empire. It is an attribute of Roman leadership he admires and tries to perfect within himself. It has been rumoured the Emperor ordered the murders of possible successors to his rule of whom he did not approve. Emperor Tiberius conducts a masterful reign of terror from behind his closed walls.

The shriek of a piglet being sacrificed jars Brutus' attention back to the activities in the Temple.

Brutus is not fond of all the many festivals that Rome celebrates, but Saturnalia particularly amuses him. Soon the wine will take effect and the dice will be tossed. Fate will take over. Someone will be made Saturnalia King for the evening. Anyone from the Emperor (if he is present) to a slave, whomever the dice favored, must be obeyed. The absurdity of the designated king's requests was always proportional to the consumption of wine. He is thankful the silliness and ridiculous clothing everyone wears only last for a few days.

Gifts are set aside along the wall for safekeeping. Caged song birds are chirping beside the candles, symbolic of the sun's return to re-awaken the dormant lands. Fruits, symbols of the anticipated fertility of the land, are aplenty, as well as colorful dolls, symbols of past human sacrifices to the gods. These gifts will be enjoyed by all throughout the days of feasting.

The traditional release of a prisoner always amuses Brutus. Who would it be this year, he wonders. Someone from his court? Such generosity is so contrary to the barbaric roots of Rome. It amazes Brutus, for he knows the person will not be free for long. Being a criminal, it is his nature to commit crimes. Even if he approaches the Vestal Virgins for forgiveness of his crimes, he will be caught again and sacrificed at the next Emperor Games, much to the delight of the excitable crowd. The bloodshed of another is always cheered and relished by all at the Circus Maximus.

Brutus reflects on ancient years. This time of year was when reigning kings would be reinvested of their power by the local priests. Their kingdom is temporarily removed from them, symbolically. The kings will declare their immunity to mistakes, and then have their kingdoms restored. To Brutus, this ritual just makes the priests think they were the true kings. He wonders how many ancient priests had tried to overthrow the local king.

Brutus always grows restless by Day Three of the festival. Too much recklessness, too much drunkenness, too many naked singers, too many people dumped into the cold Tiber River. He longs for normalcy to return. It will be four more days. To stop business, schools and the courts for these festivals, he believes, is not beneficial to Rome. It is even illegal to declare war during Saturnalia. Brutus wonders how this might anger Mars, the God of war. Not a god Brutus wants to upset.

Thinking of the gods, the time to offer evening libations to Jupiter and the Penates at his lararium is approaching. Brutus again questions his loyalty to these customs. He sees little need for such offerings, except to Jupiter on occasion.

Musing over these reflections, Brutus leaves the Temple. He walks down the odd number of stone steps, a tradition to ensure one enters the temple on the correct foot, past the twelve bronze tablets inscribed with Roman law, and onto the stone streets lined with fig trees. He walks slowly towards his large multi-roomed domus, smiling at the revellers, some women dressed as men and some men dressed as women.

He can see candles flickering in the numerous small rooms of the crowded multi-floored insulae. Every unit has several people singing and feeling the effects of too much merriment. He cannot imagine how one would sleep at all in such a building, let alone find time to pray before the small lararia that are in every household.

He passes a makeshift altar adorned with rosemary, juniper and cedar, a bonfire burning before it. He sees the Priestess walking in a circle around the fire, pausing at the four points of the cross that symbolize the position of the moving sun through the heavens. The first point where day equals night, the second place where the days are the longest, the next point with the day again equal to the night and then now, when the night is longest. When she reaches the head of the shortest leg of the cross, she chants the song of all the ages: "We celebrate the end of the longest and darkest night and welcome the new sun born of Mother Earth. Bring us the new light, the light of your glorious son. You have created life from death, bring us warmth and deliver us from the cold." Brutus moves on; he has heard the ceremony many times and is not interested in such musing of the sun-worshippers.

Suddenly he remembers there are some new young attendants at the bath. He changes direction. The bequests and gifts to the gods and the departed can wait. He needs some familiar sinister entertainment of his own to celebrate his approaching first anniversary as a Roman magistrate.

Brutus is sure the deceased ancestors will understand the distraction of festivals; Jupiter will be acknowledged with more offerings if necessary. He is growing weary of all the daily visits to the lararium anyway. He feels less need to participate in such rituals, no matter how deeply rooted in Roman custom and tradition. He would rather not have to share his wine and bread with anyone deceased—divine or mortal. His days in the court have shown how he, not just the gods, can be masters of the fate of others. He alone can determine whether a man goes free or is put to death. He does not hear from the gods in his court, nor does he consult them. He alone makes the decisions. The gods seem to have little influence in his life. Why does he bother to address them on a daily basis as do the slaves and non-working foreigners in Rome? He is superior to these people; he understands fate is to be mastered, not endured. He is one of the chosen men with power in Rome. He is to be feared just as much as the gods.

He enters the warm moist confines of the bath with eager anticipation of exerting his dominance.

SOUTHEAST OF PALMYRA, SYRIA

Discontentment soon takes hold of Jeshua at Palmyra. His skills are useful; however, his spirit is restless. He needs to roam. The solution is to work with a camel team that travels the trade route to the southeast. He ventures four stops along the spice route in the direction of India. Occasionally the team will travel to the seaport at the tip of the Arabian Peninsula. Jeshua finds the work challenging and interesting. When they reach areas inhabited by people from India, he starts to hear a very different philosophy from what he had heard at the Temple in Jerusalem during Passover. This intrigues his spirit.

A man known as the Buddha had been born into luxury in northern India some six hundred years before. The son of the local King, he had married at the age of sixteen, which was the custom, and lived within the lavish confines of the palace grounds. When as a young man in his late twenties he was able to venture out of his royal residence, he was appalled at the poverty and suffering he witnessed surrounding his manor.

He immediately gave up his privileged life and began to search for a way to relieve this suffering. He tried abstinence from material goods, including food, and almost died. He then tried meditation. After some experimenting with focused thought, he decided to continuously meditate for over forty days. His colleagues left him alone under a tree. One day, while meditating under that tree, a solution appeared to him. From that day on, he dedicated his life to that of a teacher, spreading the knowledge he had received.

His message was that appeasing gods with rituals and sacrifices was not the way to relieve mortal suffering. Rather, it was achieved through personal choice and self-responsibility. He presented his Four Noble Truths. Firstly, life was suffering. Not just illness or poverty, but also pleasure and enjoying good things. For these were temporary and the more we enjoy, the more we miss and therefore suffer. Secondly, our suffering was caused by desire, thirst or greed and our desires would always exceed our resources. To relieve our discomforts and fulfill our desires, we were always looking outside ourselves. This was not the way. The Third Noble Truth addressed this. To stop suffering we needed to stop desires. This is done by not becoming attached to our desires. We must also not place our self-identity with places we visit or ideas we entertain, such as cultural traditions. We needed to practice non-attachment with everything, even our bodies. We must accept the fact that we all get old, decay and die. Fourthly, we should practice the Eightfold path and embrace the middle way. Just believing in a doctrine was not useful; one must live it and work with it to gain benefits.

Jeshua thinks to himself … suffering from a Jewish point of view is a result of an angry god who must be appeased. The Roman population is always offering sacrifices to their ancestors and gods. It is a compelling aspect of daily life. The lives of all throughout the Mediterranean revolve around appeasing the gods, whatever their culture or tradition, be it Greek, Egyptian, Roman or Hebrew. That is the way to a peaceful life.

The words of this Buddha are very powerful for Jeshua. He feels drawn to the ideas and wants to learn more. Ever since the Angel visited him, he has known that a daily focus of appeasing the gods was false. He has never heard any philosophy like this. Yes, there are Greek schools, but they still address the myths of their culture. The Greeks believe knowledge and wisdom are the route to happiness. However, the Buddha's ideas for obtaining knowledge are to eliminate personal suffering to create a peaceful life, not for atonement with an angry or unpredictable deity.

His mind and soul wonder what it would be like to visit India. He starts to put a plan in place. He needs to discover a way to follow the trade routes and sail to Goa or Debal on the northwestern coast of India. His spirit soars with excitement. His hidden Angel of Light seems to be pointing the way. His heart is filled with anticipation and joy.

INDIAN SEAPORT DEBAL
18 A.D.

A spice cargo ship returning to its home port of Debal is the perfect vehicle for Jeshua's journey to India. Upon arrival, his first chore is to find passage to northern India. His destination is Lumbini, just south of the grand mountains, the Himalayas. This is the birthplace of the Buddha. His enquiries reveal the land route to be long and arduous. There is a huge desert to cross and mountains beyond that present challenges. The chances of delays are numerous. He decides to locate sea passage to northeastern India via a boat that travels to the seaport Tamralipti by the mouth of the Ganges River. From there, he can find a river boat sailing up the Ganges, and then a short land passage to Lumbini.

As he nears his destination, he is awestruck by the natural beauty of the area—magnificent mountains cradling the white clouds giving way to lush green plains supporting an unbelievable variety of birds and animals. He has not seen anything like this in the dry deserts and rocky hills of his homeland or his travels.

There are many shrines and monasteries erected to this wonderful teacher. As he approaches the sacred gardens of Lumbini, Jeshua can see the pillar erected by King Asoka marking the birth place of the Buddha. It has stood for almost three hundred years.

After his first military engagement, the King Emperor had been so shaken by the post-battle destruction and suffering he witnessed that he immediately vowed a non-violent life. He implemented a national policy that followed the Buddha's teachings. He sent envoys out to the known world in China and the Middle East. However, his efforts to spread the philosophy did not have a large impact. Shortly after his death, India went a different way.

Jeshua finds a monastery close to the gardens to rest. The monks are friendly and offer a warm welcome. He soon fits in with his carpentry skills, doing repairs that are needed. Shortly after his arrival, he begins to accompany the monks on their morning meditations. This is all new to him. During his meditation, he can quiet his body but his mind dances about. He often recalls his journey to this peaceful place by the mountains or ponders upon what food he will eat next. Sometimes his mind just seems to meander with little continuity of thought.

He hears more about the middle way and the Eightfold Path. The middle way is how Buddha described a way of life that was between the excessive opulence of his youth and the self-denial and deprivation of his adult journey to enlightenment. The extremes practiced in his culture need to be avoided for the middle way to be maintained. Adequate nourishment of the body and its senses is a necessity for living the Eightfold path. Doctrines must not just be believed but must be followed and practiced. The Eightfold path comprises wise or right understanding, right thought, right speech, wise actions, right livelihood, wise effort, right mindfulness and right concentration. In other words, life is to be lived and enjoyed through taking self-responsibility.

The monks speak about suffering. Life is suffering. Suffering is not only illness and discomfort. It also results from our desires that are driven by the physical senses of our bodies. When our eyes see a pleasing scene, we desire to see it again. When we hear a beautiful sound, we desire to hear it again. In between, we long for what we desire. We can eliminate this suffering by studying the ways of our bodies, minds and hearts. We must become aware of these aspects of our existence.

The monks speak that our true selves are not our bodies, for they are youthful, grow old and then decay. Nothing is permanent but rather ever-changing. It is impossible to control anything. The desires of our senses and bodies need to be witnessed by our inner self, our observer mind. These desires must be viewed as incidents unrelated to who we are. Our minds are also not our real selves but a series of changing and fluctuating thoughts. One moment we are thinking about a friend and then abruptly we focus on a task that needs to be done. Our hearts behave in the same fashion, feeling joy and quickly shifting to anger after some interruption of our joy.

Jeshua learned we must develop mindfulness, the ability to observe our body, mind and heart, and expand the observer mind within us. We must examine all the ways the body demands attention and detach from these demands. We must observe what the mind and heart do as well. Let them play as if they are unsupervised children. Become acquainted with all their expressions. This mindfulness will reveal all there is to know about the body, mind and heart. The subtle mind will become the observer and the observed. When the mind sees anger or greed appear, it will allow them to pass through without attachment. When desires of the physical sense rear up, they will be observed for what they are, temporary demands. When one feels anger or greed, one will realize this too will pass. This is correct concentration and the wisdom that the Buddha teaches—Samadhi. This stability of mind occurs when one sees the body, mind and heart as if at a distance, as an unbiased observer, seeing them as they really are, not permanent parts of existence but variable and temporary aspects of life.

When the body, mind and heart become an observed quality, they are no longer a part of us. They are separate from our experience, somewhat like observing the clouds dropping rain upon a mountain. We observe this but it is not of us. We realize we are more than these happenings. They are aggregates of phenomena, not of our true permanent selves.

Each morning one sits quietly and concentrates to bring forth the observer mind, the inner sun. Concentrating the mind onto the flow of breath entering and leaving the body is one way to achieve this stillness of observation. This equips a person with the right mindfulness to live the day with wise thoughts and actions, an acquired skill that comes with much practice. In the moment the observer mind sees that all is totally detached, Nirvana or bliss is temporarily experienced. The mind will fall back until the next moment of perception, which will last a bit longer. This gets easier with each repetition.

Jeshua studies and absorbs the ways of the Buddha. He starts every day with purposeful meditation. He practices observing the behavior of his body, mind and heart as he goes about his daily tasks. He becomes adept at observing the components that make up his temporary life. Joy and awe fill his being. He finds spiritual freedom and completeness. The moments of Nirvana are beyond description. They remind him of being in the presence of his Angel. The idea of a vengeful God leaves his consciousness forever. The concept of appeasement vanishes.

~

Four years passed quickly. The time had come to consult the sacred circle. Jeshua thanked his gracious hosts. They appreciated the fine repairs he had done to the monastery. He began the long journey home. The sojourn seemed to pass quickly.

It was Peterus, the chief elder of the village, who first saw Jeshua approaching the village. A celebration was quickly arranged. Thomas, the teacher, excused the children from their studies and they all raced towards the seashore to play. James was full of questions for his brother. The elders listened closely. After a delightful feast and homecoming, Jeshua followed his heart to the scared circle.

The night sky was clear and dark; the stars were brilliant as the new moon was not visible. The Star of Knowing was resting at his shoulder. Jeshua fell into a light sleep. The stunningly beautiful celestial Angel appeared again, surrounded by brilliant silver pulsating light. Her presence was filled with compassion and infinite joy. Jeshua was awestruck, as usual. The message she brought was that he was nearing his true mission in life; however, he must first spend time at the Museum in Alexandria Egypt. The knowledge he will gain there will deepen his resolve to follow his heart. Jeshua wasted no time lingering in his village. He bade all farewell and assured them he would return in seven years.

ALEXANDRIA, EGYPT
22 A.D.

Jeshua arrived at the Canopic gate in the eastern walls surrounding the city of Alexandria. He paid the toll to enter the city and was immediately in the Jewish district. It was behind the Royal Palaces and stretched out to cover about a quarter of the size of the area inside the walls. The trade from India, China and Arabia had fuelled the success of his people here. Jeshua easily found accommodation and was offered work immediately. He did carpentry to gain income and soon located the Museum.

There he discovered the library and was amazed at the extent of the knowledge that was stored there. He learned of the copy room where all books that flowed through Alexandria on the ships were removed and copied. He volunteered to work there. Soon the books consumed his entire time. To be able to read so much interesting material was thrilling. Greek philosophy, astronomy, engineering, medicine, agriculture and history were but a few of the topics he was exposed to and reproduced.

The first summer he was grateful to be working within the cool of the stone walls of the Museum. He appreciated the evenings sitting in the shaded gardens surrounding the library. He often had conversations with the scholars who were studying and working there. It was a menagerie of intelligence and forward thinking. Jeshua was very much at peace with himself.

One evening while sitting alone, he noticed a young woman approaching. He had seen her before. She was charming and occasionally worked in the copy area. She seemed to be Jewish but he had heard her speaking Latin from time to time. Most spoke Greek in the Museum. However, knowledge of languages was a requirement to work there. He asked her to sit with him. She did.

He discovered that it was also her first summer in Egypt. She too was grateful to be working indoors at the Museum, sheltered from the relentless summer sun. She enjoyed her evenings strolling through the gardens and sitting under the Nahet trees. There she also discussed ideas with scholars from Greece and Syria. She enjoyed the aroma of the pine and cedar trees permeating the gardens. She watched the lotus flowers close as the evening daylight faded into the darkness of night.

Jeshua started talking about his work in the copy room. He felt it ironic that he was translating Cicero's writings into Greek, when it was he who had translated Greek Philosophy to Latin so the Romans would be introduced to a more philosophical way of life.

Soon he inquired how she came to live in Alexandria. She told him she had arrived by sea from Italy in the spring. The crossing had been exciting. It was early in the shipping season when latent winter winds often cause storms at sea. Jeshua listened intently as she described the ship being tossed about by the waves. In spite of the rough seas, she found the passage thrilled her adventurous spirit. Jeshua sensed the excitement of her experience in his own heart. He knew they would be friends. Her name was Maria.

Soon they were spending most evenings together in the garden. He shared Cicero's view of True Law. True Law was in agreement with nature, unchanging and everlasting. Rome's preoccupation with the military, governance and matters of Roman law was misguided. True Law did not command an adherence or obligation declared by man, whether Emperor, Senate or religious leaders. The laws of man differed between Greece, Rome and Palestine. True Law, however, applied to all nations. There was one Master, one Truth, which was God, our Creator. To not honor this True Law was to deny our divinely human nature. Jeshua agreed with Cicero.

Jeshua also told her of his time in India and how he had studied the ways of the Buddha. He practiced mental concentration. He had been touched by Nirvana. He found it interesting that two people from two completely different cultures had arrived at the same conclusions about life and death. Cicero and Buddha both shared the same observations about people and Creation. There was one natural spiritual force. It was available to all with proper attitude, wise intention, words and actions. It was above all rules, laws and dictates of men and their leaders. It could not be controlled or manipulated.

Before long, Jeshua and Maria met in the garden every evening. He discussed the books he was working with. They often marvelled at how parchment was so much better and easier to work with than the papyri scrolls. These codices could be written on both sides, making the task much easier to complete. It also made for more compact storage as the library had already been expanded to include another large building.

Jeshua learned that Maria was very interested in maintaining one's health through the use of muscle manipulation, healing oils and herbs. She had studied at the medical school founded by Hippocrates in Kos, Greece. She believed in his philosophy for health which involved observing both the patient and his environment, not just looking for different unrelated diseases as other Greek medical schools taught. She then had gone to Rome for continued practical experience. The health of the Roman legions was an ongoing concern. She worked with the warriors to maintain their vigor and help them recover from injuries using massage, herbs and oils. She was adept at simple surgeries to treat battlefield wounds, such as removing arrow heads, while at the same time maintaining the warrior's health. She was versed in the latest techniques of the laying on of hands and participated in the sessions that were held every week at the research center of the School of Greek Medicine at the Museum. She translated some of the procedures from the Corpus Hippocraticum manual into the current Greek language in the copy room. That was why Jeshua saw her there from time to time.

They started to spend time together away from the Museum. They took short trips to the markets, even to Cairo. Eventually they were inseparable. They began travelling farther distances. They got to know each other more. She learned more about Jeshua's years travelling the spice roads. He liked to be among people. He enjoyed those who seek Truth. He learned that Maria was passionate about the health of the human body.

They decided to take a journey together and explore Upper Egypt. She had never been sailing on a river, just the sea. It would be exciting. The ideal time to take their adventure was when the summer heat broke.

In the cool air, they met early in the morning before sunrise. It was always a scramble to find a boat going south out of the delta. They looked for a cargo ship loaded with lumber for construction of tombs and temples. Egypt was one of the most fertile lands of the Mediterranean with one curse—few trees. This led to the pharaohs importing trees and planting ebony, pine, and cedar trees, species that were especially useful for building boats. Egypt cultivated papyrus in the jungles of the delta which was exported to the world.

Maria and Jeshua found a freight boat that would take them past the delta and all the way to Thebes. They watched the captain with his long wooden pole. He was standing at the bow of the boat repeatedly digging the pole into the bottom of the river. Each year floods would change the sandbars and shoals, making it easier to run aground. The captain was constantly telling the oarsman at the back which way to steer the boat. Once out of the delta and onto the great river, the sails were hoisted. When travelling upstream the winds were always a blessing.

They passed fishermen on papyrus rafts using nets woven from thin willow tree branches to catch fish. Boats with royalty would glide by, maidens singing and rowing, with no intended destination. Food was being prepared on the upper deck for the royal feast. Small children were dangled over the sides of the boat watching the water dance and rush down the hull sliding through the water.

Just north of Thebes, the great river took a sharp turn east. The black fertile land was very narrow. The inhospitable red land could be seen in the distance with its sand and rocky canyons carved out of the stone. It seemed ancient rivers had chiselled through the stone, creating a labyrinth of canyons not unlike branches of a tree. One could get lost very easily walking in these canyons. The floods could be higher here than other areas. The Nile overflowed its banks every year and then retreated leaving the black silt behind. This is where the farmers tilled the soil and planted wheat and barley. Crocodiles would occasionally get stranded at the edge of the red land after the water receded. Therefore, farmers had be careful working the black land after a flood.

Maria and Jeshua disembarked at Thebes, a center teeming with activity. They longed for the quiet of the country. They went to the market to buy provisions of dried fish, olives, figs and beer then headed towards the quiet red land. The floodwaters of the Nile never reached that far to give life to the soil.

The red land seemed to be preserved forever. The heat of the desert permeated everything. Here the decomposition process appeared to be put on hold. When they ventured to the west side of the river they would occasionally pass ancient burial sites where the winds had swept the sand away to expose corpses buried hundreds of years before. They did not look any older than the day they had been placed there.

On the east side of the river they found a small cave in one of the canyons. This would be their resting place. They placed their food in the back and sat near the mouth of the cave. The sun set, the dark night sky was clear as usual, the cool air engulfed them.

This was Maria's favorite time of the year; the summer heat had left to make way for the cooler winter. They enjoyed their visit to this area of Egypt very much. It was relaxing and refreshing to get away from the Museum for a short time. They made it a habit to visit every year.

Maria and Jeshua were married in the Jewish quarter of Alexandria before the second summer ended. After the wedding feast, they travelled to Upper Egypt to enjoy each other's company for several days. It became their sanctuary. Maria reduced her time at the Museum to pursue her passion for wellness. She became a healer of the sick. She continued to attend the research clinic at the School of Medicine. Meanwhile, the work at the library consumed Jeshua. When he copied books about anatomy, healing or biology, he would share them with Maria. The years passed quickly. One morning during his meditation, Jeshua sensed it was time to return to his village. The Star of Knowing was beckoning, an Angel was calling.

VILLAGE 42
29 A.D.

The morning air was crisp and still. Peterus took in a deep breath as he marvelled at the seabirds gliding over the gentle waves of the ocean. It had been seven years since Jeshua had left for Alexandria. His return was expected soon. The elders would prepare a place for him on the village council.

Looking south, he saw two figures walking towards the village. As they neared, he recognized one as Jeshua. He shouted to the others and they all rushed to greet the pair enthusiastically. Jeshua's brother James showed off his son Matthos, born shortly after Jeshua's departure for Egypt. Maria was introduced to everyone as his wife. Thomas dismissed his class so all could hear the story of Jeshua's return. They were led to the community table. Food was prepared and all waited to hear of his adventures.

Jeshua described their time in Alexandria, the magnificence of the city and Museum, and all the books they had read and copied. He also told them that Maria was a healer and had a collection of health potions that would help all in Palestine, not just the villagers, live a happier life.

The elders informed Jeshua that he would now be a full member of the village council and his advice would be valued. Maria and Jeshua made their home in his former hut and quickly settled into the routines of the village.

After a few weeks, Jeshua told Maria that he needed some time to himself for a few days. With her blessing, he headed for his Temple, the wilderness near the sacred circle.

He pondered upon how his experiences of the past fourteen years had left him in a dilemma: he could not accept his Jewish traditions and at the same time live a life true to his heart. He had to find a way to assimilate back into his culture and be at peace with his soul. He reflected upon the wisdom he had been exposed to over the past several years. He recalled the Greek philosophy he had read at the Museum. Aristotle wrote that the human soul was separate from all connections to the body, needing no corporal organ for fulfillment. It was also imperishable, nothing could destroy it and it did not decay like the body. Happiness was the goal of life and one should avoid extremes. Also, there was an impulse for noble and virtuous behavior that was part of human nature. This impulse was founded on nature and developed by applying wise habits and clear reason. Aristotle referred to God as a supreme and eternal being not needing religious organization. Wisdom was the key to man's happiness.

These ideas were similar to what he had learned in India from the Buddhist monks. The body was temporary, as were the mind and heart, displaying constant fluctuations of expression. The real self was beyond these fluctuations. As much as he had learned there, he felt a connection with nature stronger than the Buddha had. The wondrous observations he made of the movements of the wind, the soaking driving rain, blinding sand storms and the dark night-time skies brought him a sense of connection to the Divine Creator. He relished those magnificent activities of nature as part of his soul.

When he was living in India, he had learned that Hinduism as a religion was based on one creative God that expressed itself in many different forms. Thus, there was much tolerance for differences among people, something he had not seen in his religious culture. The tax man was despised, perhaps for good reason, and the Romans who ruled the land were also disliked. The previous rulers over the Jews, the Greeks, were always viewed as untrustworthy. His Hebrew culture allowed for little or no tolerance of different or new ideas. He recalled Cicero's writings which proposed that religion could play a role in controlling the masses. It could be used to create fear that could be a powerful motivating force, even if the fear was based on falsehoods. He had seen this religious-based influence over people in Jerusalem during Passovers. He now knew that religious rituals keep individuals separated from their true selves.

The Passover celebrations were all about remembering the collective past of his people and looking forward to God's promise of restoring the children of Israel as rightful rulers of the Promised Land. There was no engagement of individual growth. He had studied the five books of Moses several times while in Alexandria and had sensed a message, especially in the book of Exodus, that the real word of God was pointed towards every individual, not a race of people. Even the two different books describing how Moses received the Ten Commandments disagreed with some of the details. The Temple priests hid the truth from those who could not read and restricted access to the Torah for those who could.

Jeshua saw the book of Genesis as a metaphoric description of the nature of individual human beings. The male and female were symbolic of life. Mankind was first aware of his body, the male, and then over time became aware of his soul or inner life, the female. The problem that faced mankind was when he entertained mixed, unfocused thoughts—the fluctuating mind as described by the Buddha. The key was learning to say no to the temptation of scattered mental focus, the mixed fruits. In Exodus, the Promised Land was like the land of Nirvana in Buddhism, the moment of perfect inner divine realization. There was a natural heartfelt desire for supreme joy and peace given to us by God the Creator. The tools for the journey to this supreme joy, the Promised Land, were universal spiritual principles that never waivered. These principles were revealed to mankind in the form of the Ten Gifts or Commandments. When studied beyond their literal meaning, these gifts described the mental attitudes required to reach the Promised Land, which resided within each soul. The moral code of Leviticus provided guidelines for celebrations; life was to be enjoyed, regularly. Numbers assured us that despite our mind's eagerness to control everything and dictate the ways of our life, God had the patience to wait until we realized the folly of this attitude. Deuteronomy summarized the previous chapters and reiterated that the journey of each individual's life was to his own internal Promised Land. Jeshua could see how his forefathers and the Pharisees had looked at these gifts and turned them into a religion for their personal purposes—power and control over the people. The last thing they wanted for the people was personal spiritual freedom and encouragement. They demanded total obedience to them and their Temple from the masses. Rituals and religious rules guaranteed their hold on power. Jeshua saw no use for such doctrines.

He reasoned and knew he could not control the outcomes of the lives of others; all must live their own lives. Possibly he could influence others in a positive manner. He accepted that his way was a personal inner path and resolved to settle into the village routine as much as possible. His morning meditation would no doubt attract attention. He would explain his behavior to those who asked and teach his methods of mental concentration to those who requested it. Jeshua would not dictate his ways to others, for he knew each person was the master of his own soul.

Finally, he reflected upon the visits from his Angel and her prediction for his future. While in her presence, he had envisioned large crowds listening to him speak. Despite this, he considered his mission was not for mass appeal but a one-on-one journey. His message would be that the kingdom of God is within the heart of everyone, not located in some promised land in the deserts of the eastern Mediterranean. The kingdom was overwhelmingly blissful, joyful and compassionate. It could be reached with personal effort and responsibility; no one needed another to find that place within his own heart. The tools for the journey could be found by studying the Ten Gifts of Moses. His message would be simple yet frightening to those who had dedicated their entire lives to religious traditions. Jeshua contemplated his thoughts as he walked slowly among the hills. He felt at peace.

He eyed a wild red tea bush. He picked some leaves. Maria would be pleased with his find. The red tea was rare and useful in releasing the fever that gripped some people during the winter months.

Jeshua returned to the village, happy to be back in his homeland. This was his Temple. His destiny was in order. He hoped his nephew Matthos would show some interest in his ways.

THE EASTERN
MEDITERRANEAN
30 A.D.

In a small cave next to the village, Matthos listened intently to Jeshua, his eyes focused on the unfamiliar black markings on the papyrus. At the age of seven years he was being allowed to hear and study the Lessons. His heart was racing with excitement. He had seen in the bright eyes of the others in the village the joy of living the Lessons. Jeshua had started to share his Truth with the elders and others of the village who asked. He had been right; his and Maria's morning meditation ritual had attracted a lot of attention. He was humbled when others asked about their habits. Jeshua was glad he had brought several of his favorite books from Alexandria. Thomas also enjoyed the writings.

In the distance there was a rumble, the sound of horses and chariots, the shouts of soldiers. Light brown dust rose into the hot air suspended like a low stationary cloud. Everyone quickly left the cave, being careful to hide all the papyri in the cracks between the rocks. Then the entrance was concealed with tree branches and dead brush. The head count must be right when the soldiers passed through. Last time, young Jonas stayed behind near the cave and the soldiers did not leave the village for two

63

days. Then they destroyed the village well, filling it with sand and rock before they left. The Roman legions were harsh on those who did not cooperate with Rome. They had to quickly get to the road so the soldiers would have a correct head count.

A new well was being dug, in the shape of an upside down pyramid. The men would dig deep down into the soil until water oozed from the cool sand. Stones and rock picked from the surrounding desert were piled up beside the large hole, sorted by size and shape. They were used to form a circle around the water that was collecting. Green reeds were crammed into the spaces between them to stop the sand seeping in. Large hollow reeds were laid horizontally to allow for more water to collect in the well. As the stones rose, sand was filled in to support the structure.

The soldiers stopped. They were a cohort from the local legion. They counted the villagers. "Yes, forty-two, as there should be," the Centurion yelled. The entire cohort watched and laughed at the tired bodies working under the relentless hot sun. They left as quickly as they had arrived. A cloud of choking dust drifted from the road, a relief to all that their stop was brief this time. The legions passed frequently on this road between Rome and Egypt. A few of the elders could remember when the road was quiet, before Egypt became a Roman province. Matthos disliked their visits. Every time they travelled through his small village, things changed. Apprehension gripped his community.

However, activity on the new well progressed faster after the soldiers left. When the top of the well reached the length of two adults from the surface, there was a hushed meeting among the elders. "The top of the well must be no wider than a basket," Teacher said. "We need to minimize the sand blowing into it and destroying the well too early."

Wells in this area did not last much more than a generation as they filled with sand stirred up by the winds of the storms that passed through the region.

There was a problem. They had to construct the well with a hidden compartment to conceal the papyri of the Lessons. Soldiers, it was feared, may stay at the village and find and destroy them, thinking they were fuel papyri intended for cooking. The opening of the well would be too small for any of the elders to squeeze through. They looked intently at Matthos.

ROME
30 A.D.

"Guilty!"

Brutus adores the sound of his own booming voice, emanating from the raised dais where he is seated and bouncing off the stone and wooden arches of the roof of his basilica. The statue of Jupiter beside him seems to smile upon hearing his words.

He also drinks in the terror and fear on the face of the defeated man who has just heard his verdict. This condemned person standing in front of him with a shocked look on his face draws up a deep sense of power within Brutus. The same power he feels when he has his way with the boy attendants at the bath. He relishes the moment.

"Guilty!"

Again the sound of his voice bouncing off the raised dome above him and the semicircle of concrete architecture behind seems to propel his voice down the long marble central hallway. The daily business activity beyond the stone columns of the colonnades of the basilica briefly stops, everyone looking from the long side flanks to see who has been condemned by the courts.

Brutus revels in the anguish his words evoke in the man's eyes and the faces of his family. This plebeian was caught stealing olives and grapes, delicacies from the Palace of the Victors during the August Ides celebration. "To feed my family," he had cried, trembling in the grip of the soldier who caught him. Brutus replies, "There is no need to steal when free food is available during each festival. Only a fool would enter the Palace to steal from his leaders. Move him to the prison to await deportation to Sardinia or for use in the Emperor's Games."

Brutus, now the highest Court Justice in all Rome after only thirteen years a judge, sits for a few moments and admires his court. This special edifice, the Basilica Julia in the Forum, was built in honor of Julius Caesar. It was dedicated by his holy son Augustus. It feels to Brutus as though it was built just for him. He likes to think of it as part of his reward for sparing the current Emperor's son any harshness for his many crimes throughout the Empire. The Emperor's Consuls grew tired of the spoiled son and sent him back to Rome in chains. He was treated as a common criminal until the Emperor bribed Brutus. The deal included his attendance in this honored basilica. There are also some hidden rooms beneath the building that are known only to Brutus.

~

Brutus accommodated the Emperor, but secretly he would have enjoyed the excitement of seeing fear in the eyes of the condemned son of the Emperor. Since Emperor Augustus, Brutus recalled, the sons of Emperors were called the sons of God. Brutus was addicted to creating fear. He would have immensely enjoyed generating that fear in a "Son of God". He loved the feeling of power, the feeling of domination over another person's life and destiny. The fear in the eyes of his victims excited him to the point of frenzy. He felt no shame or remorse. It was his elixir, his reason to live.

He imagined how the Emperor must feel to have power over all his subjects, noble and plebs alike. He considered his little games nothing unusual in comparison. After all, some of his prisoners were thrown to the beasts for the Emperor's entertainment during the Emperor Games.

~

Returning to the present, Brutus leaves his chair, walks down the three steps to the marble floor and pauses so the condemned man can see more clearly who has judged him. His gaze is on the slanted shafts of bright golden sunlight streaming through the windows, illuminating the hall from the high walls below the ceiling. He marvels at the engineer's skill that created such a high roof. The columns and wooden arches exude a mystical atmosphere where all can appreciate the power of Rome and her leaders. He breezes past the civil servants, bureaucrats and business attendants that comprise daily life within the walls of the basilica. He is sure all eyes are cast towards him as he struts through the center hallway.

Every Roman town in the Empire has its own basilica which is the center of commerce, government and justice. It is a hub of truth. It also serves as a large gathering place for community functions. The basilica is the center of Roman life in any town.

Brutus heads for the bath. He needs more entertainment, but first a stop at the taberna. He has heard that supplies from an Egyptian ship have arrived with some tasty eastern brew. His just reward today will be a mug of beer and then pleasures in the private room with the server.

VILLAGE 42

"Matthos, come here," Teacher said. With excitement, Matthos dashed to the group, thinking his first lesson interrupted by the soldiers' visit would resume. He heard a soft command: "Stand in the water basket." Matthos, somewhat puzzled, tentatively climbed into the basket made of tightly woven willow tree branches and papyrus reeds. To his relief, it did not collapse under his weight. "Now sit in the basket," he was instructed. Matthos, as the smallest boy in the village, did well at playing games like hide from the soldiers and curling in the sand, but now he was wondering what was happening. Why was he being sized up to the water basket for the well? He cautiously sat down on the bottom of the basket. He easily fit. The elders watched and smiled. "That is good, now go off and find more rocks," one of the elders told him. As Matthos left, he saw the chief elder Peterus pause and say, "It will work."

As the well construction consumed the entire village, Matthos wondered whether his studies of the Lessons would ever resume. A small compartment built of stone was being assembled beside the well wall. It was being connected to the well by a small passageway. Finally, at the well wall itself many stones were fitted so they could be easily removed. Extra footholds were built to store the stones. They were moved and replaced many times. It had to be perfect. The stone holds had to be strong enough to withstand the bumps and swings of the water basket full of water as well as support the weight of a boy. Shortly after the final top row of stones was securely in place, Peterus said, "Now go find Matthos."

Matthos sat in the basket and was lowered into the well a short distance. He was then instructed to crawl out of the basket and stand on the stones protruding from the well wall. He did this and the stones did not move. The elders were pleased. "Move down in the well until you come to a light colored rock." Matthos found the rock in the dim light. "Push that rock into the wall," he was told. To his surprise, it moved. "Now remove all the rocks surrounding that opening."

Matthos found they all moved with ease. Then he saw a small passageway. "Now enter the space and see where it goes," he was instructed by the elders peering down at him from the sunlit surface.

Matthos crawled to a larger cavity, a space large enough to hold several large clay pots half his height. Then suddenly he realized he could see clearly, sunlight was reflecting into the area. The passageway was built to allow for the direction of the sun. Matthos could see that the other side of the well was in shadow. "Crawl back to the basket and put all the stones back, carefully," Matthos heard an elder say. He tried to remember the order in which he had removed the stones. Eventually, they were all in place and secure. He climbed up the footholds of protruding rock and emerged into the bright sunlight. As his eyes recovered from the darkness of the well, he could see Teacher smiling at him.

"Matthos, we now have time to continue your long delayed studies." Teacher then added, "From now on, you will be the Protector of the Lessons."

THE NEXT DAY
VILLAGE 42

Teacher began early, just after sunrise. The air under the olive tree was calm and cool from the night. Matthos was eager to hear the Lessons. He would cherish this day forever.

Teacher spoke. "When I was fifteen years old, I visited our sacred circle. During a light sleep, an Angel appeared before me. She was the most beautiful and magnificent being I had ever seen. She was filled with bliss and joy. She instructed me to live with my inner sun. She told me to get acquainted with my scared self, that spark of divinity that resides within each human heart. The alignment of the Star of Saturn also indicated it was time for me to take more responsibility for my life's direction. I stood where the keeper of the stones marked my birth. I aligned the Star of Saturn with the center mountain peak and it pointed to my feet. I knew the time had come."

Teacher paused for a moment, a smile on his face. "Ever since I was seven years old, the age you are now, my parents would take me to the Passover celebrations at the Temple in Jerusalem. Hundreds of thousands of people would be there for the festival. The Roman soldiers would always watch us very closely. Because our culture worships just one God, not like the Romans who adore many gods, our people are considered to be corrupt and threatening.

We were viewed with suspicion and aversion. The Greeks, when they ruled over Judea, also felt this way; to them the Hebrew people were a tribe of untrustworthy misfits. That is why there have been armed skirmishes between the Greeks and Jewish people in the past. However, the High Priest and priesthood of the Temple of Jerusalem, the Sadducees, in order to protect their positions of political power, feel it is important to cooperate with the Roman occupiers of Judea as well as pay the hated road tolls and taxes.

"Even though they built their towns on our lands and sent some of our men to Rome to be slaves, they have allowed us to continue our traditions and culture. While in Jerusalem I would often sit with the judges and scribes and listen to our history. I learned much about our people. The Pharisees held a different point of view than the Sadducees towards the occupying Roman officials. They considered themselves the guardians of the divine law as set down by Moses. They did not agree with the priesthood to cooperate with the past Greeks or the current Romans who rule our land and encouraged rebellion against the authorities. However, I could not agree with them trying to occasionally rid our homeland of the occupiers or demanding slavish adherence to traditional customs. I tried to discuss this with them, but they would not listen, their opinions were inflexible. The priesthood and the Pharisees said God was vengeful and we must fear him for they had seen his wrath when our ancestors were slaves in Egypt. We as his people had to be vengeful like him to gain access to God and please him so he would protect our culture. I knew these beliefs were wrong, I knew our God is compassionate."

Teacher paused for a moment and reflected upon the history of his people, the senseless animosity between Hebrews and the occupiers of Judea over the years and the mistaken concept of a vengeful God. Matthos filled him with hope for the future. He resumed, "When I left the sacred circle that morning, I resolved to travel the trade routes for Indian spices and Chinese silk. From Palmyra in Syria, I worked as a camel driver. I visited the temples in the towns. I heard the teachings of Eastern mystics, such as Confucius and the Buddha. I read the Tao, an ancient Chinese spiritual text. I also heard the philosophy of the Greeks being discussed among the traders at the oases. These teachings said that knowledge is universal, available to all and that self-discovery and happiness were the right of all. This was unlike our leaders, who preached that only the privileged few had the right to any knowledge and that for a contented life people must follow these leaders and judges without question."

Teacher then proceeded to explain more about the history of the Hebrew people. "We have been told that our people were homeless and led out of slavery in Egypt by Moses and that we are waiting for a Messiah to save us, a Messiah who will bring us happiness by expelling the occupiers of Judea and lead us back to our home, the Promised Land. Yet, the teachings of the East say we are all responsible for ourselves, we can reduce and overcome our own miseries, and we are our own saviors. Only we, individually, can realize our inner divine spirit. This inner sacred kingdom is our savior, our own personal Messiah.

"In our holy book of Isaiah, we are told that 'unto us a child is born, a son is given, and his name shall be wonderful, counsellor, the mighty God, the everlasting father, the Prince of Peace.' The child in this story is the symbol for our inner sun, our divine flame. When we discover it, it is like the birth of a child.

"After working the trade routes, I travelled to northern India. There I studied the words of the Buddha. I learned the power of self-reliance and mental concentration. I learned one achieves a peaceful life and spiritual freedom by applying daily wise thoughts and actions that will lead to direct experiences with the divine. Long-held religious beliefs and cultural dogmas are not the way to personal happiness and liberation."

Matthos had seen Teacher sit quietly by the seashore, cross-legged with eyes closed. He had often wondered why. Now he knew this posture was a way to be still, detached from the chaotic daily activities of maintaining fire, food, and drink. He realized now that Teacher was making conscious contact with his Creator, his Spirit, his God, his child within. Teacher would soon teach Matthos how to concentrate his thoughts.

"Those years with the Buddhist monks convinced me more than ever that the Pharisees and Temple priests were wrong. Our creator is not to be feared, nor is he vengeful. He is compassion. When we seek connection with this compassion that resides within our being, we are honoring our divine self. This must be the first thing we do each morning for a peaceful day."

Teacher continued, "Upon my return to our village, I visited our sacred circle and the Star of Saturn was now on my left shoulder. I knew the time had arrived for the next step to be taken." He explained how he travelled to Alexandria in Egypt to study with the scholars at the Museum. There, all the known books were being translated to Greek at the library. This activity had been going on for two hundred years. He gained work in the copy room. It was there he met his wife Maria Magdala. Raised by the Lake of Galilee, she had left her family to study health and healing in Greece and Italy. She was also dedicated to the preservation of truth and knowledge, so when she learned of the knowledge project at the Museum, she sailed to Alexandria. They lived and studied there together for seven years. He returned to the village, bringing Maria with him as his wife.

Teacher talked about Egyptian history. "I learned how the Egyptian priests would try to make themselves look like gods. They would remove all the hair from their bodies. They would wear masks, robes and ornaments. They would dye their skin colors they thought the gods would appear as. They did this hoping to appease the gods. They believed the gods would then grant them godlike power, power that could make them leaders over other men. Eventually, all leaders of the world, whether military, government or religious, started to think that the gods bestowed power only on them.

"Alexander the Great, who founded the great city of Alexandria, did just that. After his conquest of Asia, he declared himself divine. He insisted all Greeks prostrate themselves before him. This irritated them as he was not even Greek, but a Macedonian who had been tutored by the Greek teacher Aristotle."

Matthos enjoyed hearing about the history of the world and the travels and studies of his teacher. He now understood why Teacher's wisdom was sought by many.

Teacher advised Matthos, "The Pharisees are no different than all other ignorant leaders. They claim communion with a God who excludes all others but them. Nothing can be more wrong. Everyone has access to knowledge and truth. Everyone has access into our Creator. What you must consider is to always follow your own spirit, your own inner sun. We become godlike not when power is bestowed upon us by an outside divine force. We become godlike when we see compassion as our Creator. Our messiah is inside our hearts and our personal power is in expressing this inner divine compassion. We must choose to embrace this compassion that is within us. This is very simple, yet our leaders remain ignorant, frozen in their dogma and traditions of vengeance and fear.

"Just as the sun in the sky shines on everything, excluding nothing, our inner sun shines on all of us—Romans, Hebrews, Macedonians, Greeks, Egyptians, women, slaves and even the Emperor. We are all equal and have access to our own messiah. The Messiah of our forefathers is not of flesh and blood. He is an inner awareness of the divine creative spirit within, our inner sun, our sacred self, the child within, our kingdom of heaven, Nirvana. This is our common ground, which makes us one. When we know this intellectually and emotionally, we will have found our spirit, we will have found our birthright; we will have found our promised homeland."

Teacher paused for a long time and gazed out at the calm sea, then continued. "We are all like the birds that fly along the seashore. As fledglings in the nest, we scream for food, unaware of our own wings and true potential. One day, we become aware of our wings but do not know how to use them. Eventually, we realize our birthright is not to squawk in the nest but to soar high on the wind currents across the sky. It is the same when we discover the Truth, our own inner sun. Until that moment, we defend our personal noisy squawking, which is rooted in our traditions and fears. That is why we speak of this Truth in parables, that each individual can discover his own wings. It is a personal journey. Only you can spread your wings, no other savior or messiah can do that for you. Look upon nature and it will reveal yourself to you. You are a marvel of this Creation." Teacher gazed at Matthos with a warm smile; he realized Matthos understood what he was saying. He was pleased with his nephew. His student had listened well.

Teacher stood and walked to the seashore. The seabirds flew above him. A gentle onshore breeze flowed through his hair. The brilliant sun was setting in a cloudless blue sky. Yellow-orange sunbeams were dancing along the crests of the small rolling waves. The Star of Saturn shone brightly in the early night sky.

ROME

Brutus was in no hurry to get to the bath after his stop at the taberna. His favorite woman was serving beer. He lingered with her longer than usual. It cost him more.

He liked to replay the afternoon court sessions in his mind. He enjoyed recalling his deceit and treachery. He recalled the evening when the wife of the man whom he had just condemned gave herself to him on his promise to spare her husband. He relished the stunned look in her eyes as he pronounced him guilty. Each time he pronounced the prisoner guilty, his eyes would dart between the man and his wife. His arrogant, self-serving smirk was the only thing they saw. Today was a satisfying day. He had no complaints. "My power can only be matched by the Emperor or the gods," he thought to himself.

The time at the bath would be savored. It was here at the bath where he first noticed how his actions could rob people of joy and replace it with fear. He would surprise the boy attendants with his carnal desires as they turned their backs to him. Then the young girls in the drying room would also be subjected to his self-serving pleasures. His only regret was that the overseers of the baths did not change the boys and girls with new offerings more frequently. Some days no attendants could be found. Today was one of those days; he felt let down. He had looked forward to more self-serving sadistic adventures. Some of his swagger vanished. "I must take this up with the Emperor," he thought to himself as he slipped his tired body into the warm water. "After all, he is a son of God."

"The pleasures of Rome are disappearing. In the past there were always plenty of attendants and delicacies at the baths. Beer and wine were available in the side rooms, as well as women offering their sensual services. Something needs to be done to bring the pleasures back," Brutus said out loud. "Where are you, Jupiter? Have I not sacrificed enough saffron for your needs? I await your generosity." Brutus seemed to have overstepped his own authority by questioning the gods. He fell silent.

VILLAGE 42

Matthos sat cross-legged on the ground under the shade of the olive tree. His eyes closed, he was practising thought concentration as Teacher had taught him and he was progressing. Teacher sat across from him and waited for his student to emerge from his celestial sphere. When he opened his eyes another lesson was imminent.

When with Teacher, Matthos felt a sense of peace, joy and depth of spirit. A sense he did not feel in the presence of anyone else, even the High Priest in the Temple of Jerusalem during Passover.

Jeshua began, "Last session, I spoke of the Star of Saturn, also called the Star of Knowing. When you were born, the keeper of the stones walked to our sacred circle. He approached the mountain peak and looked in a circular fashion until he could see the Star of Saturn. It is the furthest planet from the earth, the jumping-off point for entry into the heavens. With his eyes firmly aligned on the peak and the planet, he set into the ground stones marking your birth. Since then, every time the moon disappeared for three sunrises, the keeper placed a pebble into a goat skin sac. This sac is now yours." Teacher handed Matthos an embroidered sac made of goat skin and dried reeds and stained yellowish-purple. The yellow was from the saffron crocus flower and the purple from the murex sea snail. It was magnificent.

Teacher explained the importance of paying attention to the pebbles in the goat skin sac. "It contains eighty-nine pebbles, representing the number of new moons that have passed since your birth." As this is often difficult to track, Matthos was told he could change the pebbles to represent sun years. This would mean his sac would now contain only seven small stones. Or, if he no longer wished to keep track with the sac, he could return to the sacred circle of the village and find in the ground the stones marking his birth. He could then align the mountain peak with the Star of Saturn and determine where he was in his life's progression.

Teacher explained to Matthos that the planet Saturn was his life guide. "At every seven sun cycles, if you return to the sacred circle and stand on the stones marking your birth, you will see that the Star of Knowing has moved. Saturn, now seven years after your birth, is aligned with your right shoulder. In the next seven sun years, it will be aligned with your feet, the next seven sun years with your left shoulder. Seven sun years later it will appear to return to the point of your birth. Each of these points represents a time to examine your life, to reflect on your relationships with people and all living things, to contemplate on how you have taken responsibility for your time and upon your connection with what the Lessons have taught you."

Despite his initial enthusiasm, the Lessons seemed rather boring to Matthos, who really was waiting to be old and big enough to go out in the fishing boats. He wanted to help with the gathering of fish to feed the villagers and travelling guests. He was just a boy who enjoyed the carefree life of exploring and watching the happenings around the village. However, he continued to listen.

Jeshua revealed to Matthos that there was an inner spiritual sun within his being, a spirit that was like the sun that shines in the sky. That sun provided the warmth for life and nourishment to all physical creation. This inner sun provided spiritual nourishment to his inner self and gave the necessary nourishment to his entire body and all its functions. Every human being possessed the same inner sun. Though confusing to Matthos, he could see the joy in the elders and villagers who understood the Lessons and lived by that wisdom. He longed for that same joy.

"The inner sun is rooted in the same essence of what created the stars and the earth, the sea and the wind, and all the birds and animals," Teacher said. "Each visit from the Star of Saturn at the angles of your body as I explained—angles like a cross—signifies a time for self-examination. Look for better ways to align your physical activities of living with your inner sun," Teacher instructed.

Teacher then unrolled a papyrus scroll. To Matthos, it was covered in nondescript black scratching that looked like patterns he made in the wet sand with a branch from a small bush.

Teacher told Matthos the elders had been observing him since his birth. They saw that he was patient, different from the other boys. They felt he would make a good pupil for Teacher to teach how to write. He would be Teacher's special student. Thomas had agreed. Matthos would learn what the papyrus was saying. If he enjoyed the Lessons, it would be his decision, his decision only, whether to become a village scribe. It did not matter what the elders thought. Matthos answered immediately, "I want to learn. I will probably never be big or strong enough to handle the fishing nets. This will be fun."

Over the next several weeks, Matthos would be taught the elements that combine to make the scratching on the papyrus turn into stories. He would be thrilled beyond his imagination. He would come to understand that the scratching on the papyrus had been made by other human beings who were communicating with Teacher and himself.

Matthos also learned more about the great Museum of Alexandria in Egypt where Jeshua had studied. The Museum had many study halls and beautiful gardens. It was visited by all the great scholars of Greece and the Roman Empire in all fields of human endeavors such as medicine, geography, astronomy, spiritual rituals, cooking, history and engineering. The Museum was also the location of the great library of all knowledge, which housed a collection of papyrus scrolls of all the known books in existence. Teacher said that since it had become difficult to obtain enough papyrus, parchment was being experimented with to create new books. He explained that every ship that docked in Alexandria was inspected by port officials. Any books on board were removed to be copied at the Museum by people just like himself and then returned to the ships.

Matthos was enthused to learn more about Alexandria and the Lessons. His day with Teacher passed quickly. The sun was falling into the calm sea. They walked to the seashore and watched the last light of day turn into dusk. It was a clear moonless evening. A new beginning was emerging. Teacher was smiling.

SUN RISE
VILLAGE 42

Dawn breaks early, it seems. Matthos is about to charge to the sea and play along the shore. He likes to chase the seagulls and feel the damp sand on his feet just as the waves recede. He enjoys the cool of the morning before the heat from the sun bakes the sand dry. This is how he always starts his day. Today, however, he knows, is the beginning of his new life. He will learn the Lessons and become a scribe. He goes to the olive tree and sits under the shading branches, thinking about what Teacher told him. He crosses his legs, sits straight, closes his eyes and concentrates on his morning meditation.

When Jeshua appears, he seems disturbed. He looks very concerned. He begins the lesson but appears to be distracted. Matthos asks if he is concerned about the soldiers who stop at the village from time to time. There is no reply. Jeshua gazes out to sea. His thoughts seem far away. His face is not showing joy today. He stops the lesson and sends Matthos to the seashore to play.

EASTERN
MEDITERRANEAN

Teacher and the elders were walking along the seaside road. They were headed to the next village to trade fish for papyri. This village had supplied them with water after their well had been destroyed. The elders were questioning Teacher, as usual. He was growing weary of the elders' constant pressure. He did not desire to be viewed as anything more than a teacher. Leader, savior—and especially Messiah—were not his desired destiny.

"You must share your pathways, your knowledge, your understanding and your gentleness. Look at how much Matthos has changed since you began tutoring him," Peterus stated. "Your philosophy and knowledge will save our people from themselves and their history." All the other elders shared his position. They pleaded with Jeshua to listen to them. They said his understanding of life must be spread to all of their people, not just the elders and one boy.

Early that evening, as the sun was fading to the dark of the night, the elders returned to their village. Jeshua walked through the pleasant night air to the sacred circle. He found the place that marked his birth and aligned the Star of Knowing with the mountain top. It was now at the same place in the sky as it had been at his birth. The Star of Knowing, Saturn, had completed one cycle. He recalled the first visit from the Angel fifteen years earlier. The sense of pure bliss and joy from her presence filled his entire being again. He knew it was time. He fell into a light sleep. The Angel appeared. Her radiant beauty surrounded by brilliant white light again filled him with bliss and joy. She smiled; her brilliant bright eyes stared directly into his heart. She faded away slowly.

NEXT DAY
PALESTINE

Jeshua returned to the village early the next morning. He called the elders together. He told them he had spent the night at the sacred circle and the message he had received was to share his knowledge beyond their village. He indicated he would follow the wishes of the elders, but only to be a teacher, not their leader, and most certainly not their savior or Messiah.

The teaching of the Lessons was a part of his spiritual pathway. He had sensed this over the past fifteen years while in Syria along the spice trade routes and while studying in India and Alexandria. He now knew what the Angel meant by his apprenticeship with spirit. Jeshua decided to give lessons only during the full moon. He chose this time because it was when the sacred energy was strongest for self-realization. The light was at its fullest expression. It was symbolic of seeing one's way clearly.

Teacher contemplated upon the Lessons. He could speak of the temples he had visited and the wisdom he had heard during his time in northern India. He could speak of the different spiritual and philosophical disciplines he had studied in Egypt. However, he wanted to do more than just share his travels with others. He wished to point out to people the limitations of the ideas preached at the Temple in Jerusalem, limitations he had known in his heart since he was a boy. He had come to know that each individual has the means to improve his life, get out of the troubles he is experiencing. The way was not to struggle with things outside oneself, or by feeble attempts at pleasing any god, but to apply simple spiritual truths to one's life; simple but not easy. These differed from the ideas being spread by the Pharisees in Jerusalem and throughout Palestine. He knew his message would stir controversy.

When the first full moon appeared following his decision to teach, he started the first lesson a short distance from the village at an olive grove. Peterus, Matthos, Maria, his brother James, Thomas, and a few members from the next village were there. Teacher sat beneath an olive tree and observed the fading full moon in the day sky. Closing his eyes, he centered himself for a few moments and began.

"The Judges tell us that only they know the source of all truth. They tell us the only way out of the sufferings and troubles of life is to blindly obey the traditions of our forefathers. The Pharisees also focus on vengeance. If you are harmed, you must return the harm. They say this is the way of God and the way to gain his approval. But I know this is not the way to peaceful living. This is not the way of Truth. This is not the way of our Creator, our Father of spirit. Our God is of kindness and compassion, not vengeance. Vengeance is a cause perpetrated by mankind. Also, blindly following religious traditions will only keep this magnificence hidden from you."

He paused so the audience could grasp his words then resumed, "The principles of the East are very different from our priests' pathways. In the Indian temples I learned that the teachings of our nation are based on an unknowing, an ignorance of spirit and truth. When spirit and truth are discovered and unveiled to each individual, these outdated and false ideas will evaporate. Just as the physical sun removes the morning fog, the inner sun, when acknowledged, will remove the inner fog of incorrect belief. The inner sun gives life to our bodies and everything we think and create. The Promised Land or the Kingdom of Heaven is within the hearts of each and every one."

Teacher ended the first session; he wanted his listeners to ponder on this concept. He knew it was foreign and not everyone would want to abandon the ways of their ancestors and traditions. His culture viewed God as outside of the human dimension, who would deliver them to the Promised Land somewhere in the desert. He was saying the opposite. Our Creator was found within the heart of each and every being. The Promised Land was a state of being or awareness one could achieve by following the True laws of Nature, the laws of the Creator. He acknowledged the comfort the past brings to current life and its value for stable cultures. However, he also knew it was smothering the individual spirit. Each person needed to learn that a life of health, happiness and true self-expression is created by a connection with his inner divine source.

Jeshua walked quietly back to the village. The elders said he was opening up the minds and hearts of the people. He remained silent. He thought of Matthos and realized he may have to accelerate his plan. Gatherings in any of the provinces always attracted the attention of the Roman soldiers. His fear was not for himself, for he would accept whatever fate would be decreed upon him. His concern was for the survival of Truth. The Lessons must be copied and hidden in the well. It would take some time, but he felt Matthos could work accurately and quickly. Perhaps Thomas could help when he was away from teaching the young children. The challenge would be to get enough papyri from other villages or the traders passing by.

A decade of protecting and spreading the Truth passed quickly. Teacher travelled throughout Palestine giving sessions only during the full moon. He developed a following. His brother James was always with him. Thomas and Matthos were an effective team that copied his sermons. At times Maria travelled with them and attended to any sickness among the crowds. Her medicinal herbs were as popular as Jeshua's messages. Peterus was always with him. He was the person who could sense if the soldiers or Pharisees were about to create trouble. He was excellent at steering the group away from confrontations. A flock of twelve helpers accompanied them on these journeys. They helped by making needed arrangements at the villages and cities where he gave his lectures.

Matthos recorded the teachings on papyri and parchment. He called his collection the Gospel according to Matthos. Thomas also wrote his own Gospel. Maria wrote her interpretations. Others started to record the messages of Jeshua and their understanding of the Lessons. From time to time Teacher would dictate words to Matthos. Matthos always stored a copy of everything in the chamber in the well at the village. Others worked in a cave near the village. Palestine became Jeshua's school. However, the Pharisees were never far away. Often members of the priesthood from Jerusalem were also seen in the crowd. They disliked any messages that contradicted their opinions. Teacher stopped going to the Temple in Jerusalem. His temper was always tested there.

Jeshua's message was always simple and straightforward. Every person had the freedom and responsibility to discover their divine inner sun. This was the route to a happy, trouble-free life. Constant appeasement of gods was a waste of effort and sacred life. Religious rituals were a distraction and should be avoided. Each person was the leader of his own soul. The Kingdom of Heaven was within. Matthos always enjoyed listening.

PASSOVER
31 A.D.

During the first Passover after his initial lecture, while the Jewish people of Palestine gathered in Jerusalem, Jeshua decided to travel to Alexandria. Maria was excited about returning to the city where they had met. James, Matthos and Peterus joined them. Matthos was particularly thrilled to visit the place where Teacher had spent seven years studying. Thomas felt his young students needed him in the classroom and stayed behind.

They travelled along the seaside road where the tolls were fewer and the crowds smaller. Once past the road forking to Jerusalem, the tolls were not as frequent and they had the road to themselves. During Passover and other events, the tax collectors always increased their presence. This annoyed the Jewish people greatly, as the collectors were not Roman but local contractors who had agreed to send Rome a fixed amount, but always collected far more for their own use. They were disliked and shunned by their community. Yet Jeshua always smiled and greeted them with respect. He saw past the deceit in their ways and looked at their spirit, that which makes us One. When they appeared at his teachings, he would always speak with them as if they were scholars.

The donkey cart was filled with the necessities for several days of travel. Accommodations in Alexandria were arranged so they would be staying at the home of a friend who would be away in Jerusalem. The Jewish section of Alexandria was very expansive, one of the largest outside of Palestine. During Passover, it was almost deserted.

When they approached the city from the town of Canopus to the east, the first thing they saw was the towering white marble lighthouse that stood announcing the harbor. This gigantic structure had guided ships for almost three hundred years. Jeshua always marvelled at the engineering that could shed light out over the horizon for fifty kilometres. It provided safety for the constant flow of goods between India, China, Arabia and the cities of the Mediterranean. The Roman tax collectors coveted the duties and tolls that were being collected from the non-stop commercial activity, thus Egypt was annexed as a province by Emperor Augustus for the revenue. The cost of maintaining the Roman military was extremely high. One legion of soldiers alone was almost five thousand men. Alexander the Great, founder of this majestic city, did the same to support his military campaigns and massive number of fighters. All rulers had taxed the movement of goods and people to gain the resources they needed for their Empires. Despite the burden on the merchants, Alexandria grew to a population of three hundred thousand people and became the most popular city to travel to among all Middle Eastern cities. It became a hub of many nationalities and varied activities, a cultural center for not just North Africa but all the Mediterranean. All the activities and successes revolved around the commercial trade.

Alexander the Great founded Alexandria in 331 B.C.E. He set his vision to accommodate large crowds and chariots with many horses. Thus the streets were laid out in a grid pattern and were wide and long, some stretching as long as five kilometres. Unlike other major cities in the Middle East, which were a mix of narrow lanes and uninspired buildings (especially Rome at that time) his city would be magnificent. The main street running east-west, Canopic Way, would be constructed in the same direction as the rising sun's rays on the day Alexander was born, July 20, 356 B.C.E. The architecture would be a combination of majestic and massive Egyptian monuments like the pyramids and the grace and wonder of Greek building style with its huge colonnades and intricate detail. The temples would be large and imposing and the Palaces a mixture of splendid buildings and gardens. A Museum to act as a reservoir of knowledge would be erected. All this would be financed by the taxation of the trade routes through Arabia and the Middle East. To ensure maximum profit, Alexander left the building of his city to his generals and headed north. He destroyed the port city of Tyre, just north of Galilee in Phoenicia. It was the most prosperous Phoenician port in the Eastern Mediterranean. This forced the trade through Alexandria where even larger ships could be accommodated through its two harbors. Soon, frequent shipments of grain to feed the masses were heading to Rome, which continued for more than a century. A steady supply of income from shipping duties and tolls lined the royal pockets of Alexandria.

Soon the wealth filtered down to the masses and with wealth came leisure. Art and culture began to thrive. The Museum became a hub for intellectual pursuits. Many were attracted from the entire Middle East and beyond to pursue their studies and inventions. The force pump to move water was developed here by a Greek scientist, Ktesibios, during the early days of the Museum. The pump was made of bronze and was eventually manufactured and traded worldwide. Some were used as far away as Britannia. Moving water in Egypt to irrigate crops was an ongoing concern. Just clearing silt from the irrigation canals was a full time job. Historian Strabo made this city his home after Augustus took Egypt. He stayed for many years while he recorded his work.

The head of the Museum in 200 B.C.E., a man named Eratosthenes, postulated that the earth was round and, using his wizardry in geometry, estimated the circumference to be forty six thousand kilometres. The gifted and best minds were attracted to Alexandria. The Museum became a combination of knowledge from Egypt, Greece, India, Babylon and other areas of the Middle East. A sharing of research followed. For example, the Greeks were trying to establish that the planets and the universe followed a predetermined course while the Babylonians sought to precisely predict the position of the planets and celestial events such as eclipses. When they collaborated on their studies, much was learned about the patterns of the heavens.

The studies of astronomy led to a greater understanding of the cycles of the sun and nature. When Caesar met the Egyptian Queen Cleopatra VII, she introduced him to the astronomers at the Museum. When they explained the nature of the sun cycles, Caesar changed the Roman calendar from a ten month lunar-based calendar to a twelve month solar-based calendar, thus the inception of the Julian calendar. It made much more sense and proved to be more reliable in predicting planting and harvesting times for agriculture.

The Royal Palaces standing guard over the main harbor were splendor beyond imagination. Even though Augustus plundered the Egyptian treasury to pay his war veterans after his conquest over Marcus Antonius and Cleopatra, the buildings were still inhabited and sprawling, graceful and stunning. Marble and granite were intertwined to create a colorful display. Gold gilded the entranceways and silver graced the windows. Precious stones bent the sun's rays into dazzling expressions of light. The direct passageway to the Museum allowed easy access for the daily tutoring of the royal children. Knowledge previously passed on to the privileged only, now became available to all who ventured into the library at the Museum. It contained over five hundred thousand books on every subject known to mankind, from agriculture and astronomy to medicine and spirituality. Even as a Roman province, the intelligence that had gathered in Alexandria under Greek rule was allowed to continue.

Jeshua and Maria easily found their accommodations within the Jewish district. James, Matthos and Peterus were spellbound at the sights. The district was just behind the Royal Palaces so they could sense the opulence of the city from their doorstep. After settling in and resting from their journey, they headed to the market. It was awash with Egyptian linen, Chinese silk, dried fish, smoked meats, olives, nuts, fruits and local beer. The pleasant aromas of spices and fragrances wafted through the air. The variety of nationalities was intriguing to Matthos; he had never seen such differences of attire before. He was thrilled at the diversity the city offered.

They walked to the center of the city. The street, Canopic Way, was thirty meters wide, made of granite and marble and completely straight. At the end, they proceeded through the moon gate and entered the harbor area where several boats were unloading timber from Syria and wine from Sicily. They would then be loaded with spices and cloth destined for Rome. A large ship was being filled with grain, also headed for Rome. The Royal Palace stood overlooking the harbor and the royal barges that had been used for cruising upon the Nile. They had sat neglected tied to the wharves since Cleopatra had vanished, yet the magnificence of the structures was beyond imagination.

The enormous white marble lighthouse stood guard over everything. After watching the activities for a while, they returned to the city through the moon gate. The eastern sun gate or Canopic gate through which they entered the city was visible in the distance down the long and very wide roadway.

Jeshua then led them to the library at the Museum which was close to the Jewish district. It was here that Matthos became enthralled with reading and learning. Jeshua suggested he read Cicero's writings. Cicero had translated the words of Greek philosophy schools to Latin for the Roman ruling elite. He believed that a commitment to high character and individual virtue would benefit all in the community and generate social stability. These were the guiding lights in his writings. The Roman senators did not agree with Cicero and continued to follow their way of searching for fame, fortune and wealth. However, Cicero filled his writings with the much admired principles based on the Greek traditions of Aristotle. The examination of issues from different points of view was a strength displayed by Cicero—the Greek school of thought known as the Academic Skeptics. As a lawyer and politician, Cicero assessed and re-assessed information he heard. Jeshua felt Matthos would benefit from studying such material as it would help to expand his mental perceptions. It would also open his mind to develop tolerance for differing points of view.

Jeshua would refresh his own soul with writings from the Buddha. These teachings had not been recorded until one hundred years after his death. Jeshua enjoyed reading the different recalled versions of Buddha's lessons. He realized each person must find the power of personal spirit and reason for himself.

James and Peterus were left to their own resources. Both avid history buffs, they found their place in the massive edifice. In the gardens, Matthos witnessed the animated conversations between the two as they exchanged views of past great leaders and military campaigns. They were always fascinated with the exploits of Hannibal.

Books about food, biology and medicine enthralled Maria. She also purchased frankincense, myrrh and other potions at the market to take back to the village. She practiced many healing methods throughout Palestine. After Jeshua's presentations, she often tended to those who felt unwell using her oils. Her reputation as a healer was far-reaching. She always marvelled at the healing power of the human body when it had been stimulated in the correct way. Healing herbs were always with her whenever she travelled so she could aid the sick.

The philosophy of Cicero captured Matthos' attention. He was astounded at the observations of human behavior Cicero wrote about. His emphasis on self-responsibility and studying and understanding natural law were similar to Jeshua's messages. However, Cicero's motivation was most often political. He thought that religion was useful to control human behavior and could be used as a tool for public policy. Matthos agreed with this opinion as he had seen firsthand how the Pharisees at the Temple in Jerusalem used their religion to control the behavior of the masses. The ideas he read about seemed to flow from the pages directly into his soul. His days spent at the library were enlightening. He was grateful his uncle had tutored him when he had returned from this beautiful city.

Each morning before heading to the Museum, Jeshua would walk to the garden beside the library. He would sit cross-legged under a tree and close his eyes. Matthos and the others would join him and they all sat in a circle. He would remain still for a short time under the branches of the tree. When the sun was high enough to shine into his eyes, he would end the group meditation with a short saying, expressing gratitude for the warmth of the sun and the camaraderie of his friends. Sometimes strangers would ask if they could join them. Jeshua always acknowledged the spirit in everyone and welcomed them to the circle. Matthos found these morning meditations prepared him for his day; the Truth was liberating. They were peaceful moments.

The Jewish district in Alexandria stirred back to life when the Passover celebration in Jerusalem ended. The people returned to their livelihoods. With the donkey cart loaded with supplies, Matthos, Jeshua, Maria, James and Peterus returned to their village. A new Passover tradition had begun for Matthos. He vowed he would make the journey to Alexandria every year. It was his New Jerusalem. He would cherish the annual visits to the Museum all his life. He meditated every morning in the garden. He read many books. He volunteered his ability as a scribe in the copy room. This was his calling. He found peace and happiness there. He eventually got to like the tax collectors along the route; after all, they too were human and could feel joy.

ROME
43 A.D.

The streets of Rome were alive with celebration. Emperor Claudius had returned victorious over Britannia. He had conquered a land that neither the great Caesar nor Emperor Caligula were able to defeat. Although he sent four legions to battle, as their leader he was claiming credit for the victory. The rapid building of Roman towns had already begun in the conquered land. The baths would be most impressive.

Emperor Claudius was the first Roman ruler to be born outside of Italy and also the first Emperor to be awarded power by the military. He was aware of the rumblings and dislike he had created among many members of the Senate for not following proper tradition in declaring leadership. His awkward gait and sometimes difficult speech made him a target of ridicule by many. He had already sent opposition senators to the gallows. He had to be ever vigilant. Emperor Caligula was assassinated after only three years in office. It had been rumoured that even the recluse Emperor Tiberius was disposed of on the direction of Caligula. Claudius had to keep ahead of all those who opposed him. Being Emperor in Rome could be dangerous.

Claudius firmly believed Emperor Worship had to be expanded and accelerated. Since the death of Augustus, many statues of the late Emperor's likeness had been erected. They stood beside Mars, Venus, Vesta, Saturn and all the other gods in their temples. This movement had been spearheaded throughout the Empire by the wife of Augustus, Livia, called Julia Augusta after his death. It was imperative that the Emperor be seen as equal to the gods. Each Emperor after Augustus had declared his predecessor divine and created the appropriate temple and cult. However, the subjects of Rome were still engrossed in their traditions. Their lararia were attended to every day. Burnt offerings were vaporized for use by the gods. Their ancestors had to be addressed and appeased. Appeals for cures for personal suffering and protection had to be addressed in the appropriate manner. Claudius knew the Emperor must be seen as the all-knowing deity on earth. This was key to consolidating his power. Thus, the erecting of statues of the first Emperor Augustus in all temples had to be a priority.

Claudius was uncertain of how he could guarantee the Emperor's rule would prevail over all time. The Emperor must be viewed by all citizens as supreme. Emperor worship must be entrenched into society. He recalled how the masses had rallied behind Caesar when he was murdered. This showed him that the lower class could not be ignored completely. After all, it was the masses of Rome who had buried Caesar, not the elite. They could be a formidable force. He would have to align the lower life of Rome to his favor. However, he also had to watch closely for senators who would like to dispose of him. Claudius had come to an impasse: how to manage the few but powerful senators while still winning favor with the many common citizens. He decided to consult and confide in the chief magistrate Lupus Antonius Brutus. He immediately dispatched a runner with a message for Brutus to come to the Palace.

MOUNT OF OLIVES PALESTINE

Jeshua sat cross-legged under the shade of an olive tree, his followers gathered in a semi-circle. He always admired how James and Peterus were so friendly with everyone. He set himself quickly and began speaking.

"The Pharisees and the priesthood from the Temple tell us our God is beyond us and outside of all mankind, that humans are separate from God. This is incorrect. In the Genesis book of Moses, we are told about the relationship between God and man, 'So God created man in his own image, in the image of God He created him.' In nature, like produces like. A rosebush can only produce roses; a horse cannot produce a lamb. Moses tells us we are products of a divine God. In nature the offspring is the same as the parent. Therefore, we are divine spirit as well. Our responsibility is to discover this part of ourselves. When we do, our discomforts and troubles of life vanish. This has been known in the East for hundreds of years. The Buddha called this state Nirvana.

"Again from the first book of Moses, our sacred writings tell us we have dominion over all things. We are responsible for our lives. God brought the animals to Adam and he named them. This is a metaphor for our abilities to create our environments. When we understand that our God is on our side and not to be feared—he brought the animals to

Adam—we can have control over our lives. This is a spiritual principle and when we learn the spiritual laws of life and apply them, we take responsibility for our existence. If we want happiness, health, wealth and expression of ourselves on our own terms, we must learn these laws and apply them. This is simple but not necessarily easy. We do not need kings, emperors, messiahs, high priests or cultural dictates to tell us our individual ways. We need to connect with the divine that resides within our hearts, our inner life-giving sun. The Kingdom of God is within you, seek this kingdom first and all things shall be added unto you."

Jeshua paused so everyone could contemplate what he had just said. He recognized that a new interpretation of traditions is neither easy nor necessarily desired. He continued.

"In the second book of Moses, Exodus, Ten Gifts or Commandments were delivered to us. When reflected upon and understood, these Gifts hold secrets beyond the literal interpretation that reveal these spiritual truths. Applying these principles creates a connection to our divinity. We first must realize that we are part of this wonderful marvellous Creation. We must not consider ourselves superior to anything else. We are equal in the creative force. This involves thinking wise thoughts and developing mindfulness, or the ability to observe yourself.

"The Commandment to Honor your Father and Mother has been used by the Pharisees to promote their view. They say that their words are laws as directed by God and should be honored. This is incorrect. Respect for parents and grandparents and all who came before us always makes for a supportive family and tribe. It provides stability and a peaceful atmosphere to raise children. However, upon further study of this gift from God, we see a deeper direction.

"As I said, in Genesis we are told we were made in the image of God, we have the characteristics of the father. We are compassionate and creative. How do we create? We create with our thoughts. Does every idle thought we have suddenly appear before us? No. Only those thoughts that have a polarity, father and mother, will be expressed. There must be a balance between the two. One cannot dominate the other. For example, for a sun cycle to be completed from sunrise to sunrise, the night must be experienced. The duality of day and night bring expression of the reality. The same holds true with our lives. Duality must exist for creation to take place. We see this in the birth of all animals and mankind; male and female are required for creation to occur. In this gift, the father symbolizes your thought, idea, dream or goal, and the mother is symbolic of the emotion behind that thought or idea. Only thoughts charged with balanced emotion, such as the deep-felt joy of imaging the fruition of the idea, will manifest. The idle thoughts will not appear. If you wish a dream or goal to appear in your life, you must first affirm the presence of Spirit within, imagine the goal already in your life and support that with your heart, emotion or sense of true joy. Only those thoughts or ideas that have both components involved will be created in your life. This is the secret behind this gift from Creation. Honor your Father and Mother. Duality and balance are key. This is how you bring desired change into your life as you go about your daily tasks. You must have faith in the process. Doubt and fear will chase away the result you seek."

Jeshua paused and looked at Peterus. He signalled that all was calm. There did not appear to be any agitation in the crowd. He continued.

"Each and every Commandment has an inner meaning. If you take the time to study and contemplate their true meaning, they will lead you to the discovery of your inner sacred sun. As you develop wise thoughts, the Truth will rise up inside you and, just as the morning sun chases away the darkness of the night, you will see your divine inner heavenly spirit. The Kingdom of Heaven is within."

Jeshua paused again, glanced at Peterus and then looked about the crowd; he could see the people were having difficulty grasping his message. He hoped they would at least consider the Lesson. It was contrary to generations of preaching from the Temple of Jerusalem. He could see the Pharisees in the crowd gathering together and exchanging animated whispers. However, they were not smiling. They were not agreeing with him. They were steeped in their traditions. Fear was dawning across their faces. They must retain control over the masses.

Peterus motioned it was time to finish; the authorities were growing restless. Jeshua slowly rose from his seat. He lingered with the audience. He struck up a conversation with several travelling scholars from Damascus who had also spent time in Palmyra when he was there. They exchanged reminiscing stories well into the evening. Maria was overseeing a few people who did not feel well. Her herbs were a welcome relief. At sundown, Jeshua and Maria returned to the village. When they arrived, Matthos was already in the well securing the day's words.

LAKE OF GALILEE
44 A.D.

It was always thrilling for Jeshua and Maria to visit this area of Palestine. Her family still resided by the west side of the lake. It was the only time they got to see her sisters and father. Her mother had died before she went to study in Greece and Italy. After a warm reunion, they strolled along the lakeshore to where people had gathered in anticipation of the day's teachings. Jeshua enjoyed the soft breezes and warm sunshine against his face as well as the soothing sound of water lapping the shoreline.

While Jeshua relaxed and made his personal connection with the natural beauty that surrounded them, James spoke to the crowd. It had been fifteen years since Teacher started sharing his knowledge with the people of Palestine. On occasion, he allowed his brother to address the crowd and review the Lessons. Today, James spoke briefly of the dangers of trying to hold on to past beliefs and giving up hope while learning to embrace new ways.

"If you seek understanding and wisdom, ask the divine inner sun that gives to all without restraint, and you will gain what you seek. Be assured of the receipt of your desire and do not waiver in this faith. If you hesitate, you are like a dancing wave on this magnificent lake that is driven by the wind and tossed about. You cannot receive your desire of wisdom without steadfast faith in your inner sun."

Jeshua listened to how James could express the Lessons. He was also a teacher in his own right but wished to remain in a supporting role. Jeshua appreciated the efforts his brother put into spreading the word. He had seen him sitting and writing with Matthos and Thomas after his sermons. He also reproduced the manuscripts on papyri and parchment for safe keeping. He often helped Matthos at the well. If James had been smaller in stature, Jeshua knew he would be the second person in the well.

He had been contemplating what to teach on such a beautiful day. He was enjoying his surroundings. The color of the lake, the weathered rock cliffs to the east, and the sudden winds that could blow up unexpectedly made for a memorable location. When you were in a small boat, unexpected winds on the lake could be frightening. Jeshua reflected upon how the same could be said of life. Unexpected events such as illness or business setbacks could also be unsettling. When in a state of fear, it was impossible to connect with one's inner sun. He decided a short treatise following in the same direction as what James had shared would be the lecture for the day.

He sat, set himself and addressed the gathering. "Ask, and it shall be given to you, seek and you shall find, knock and it shall be opened." As always, Jeshua paused so all could ponder his words and metaphors. He knew nothing can change in a person's life without understanding and compassion. A compassion not only for others but also for one's self. Life was truly about the relationship you develop with yourself.

He explained this short passage. "It is our duty and loyalty to the Creative Spirit to acknowledge where our good fortune originates. We must not accept shortcomings in our life. We must not remain ignorant. We must not accept blockages on the pathways to our dreams. We need to bring our God, our inner sun, into our lives, especially when we feel confused and downtrodden. Our Father God is our all-knowing parent, just as you are the provider for your children. When they are growing, they are unaware and are learning. Our spirit Father acts in the same accord. He sees beyond us as we see beyond our children. When you understand your Father God is your true provider, your inner thoughts and life are in accord with your true nature. Ask and you will receive."

Jeshua paused. He knew the people needed time to contemplate the message and the simplicity of its meaning. He rose from his sitting position and strolled among the people, smiling at everyone. Today's lecture was over. It was time to go up to the top of the cliffs.

THE EMPEROR'S PALACE

"Brutus, my friend, sit down and enjoy some delicacies from my homeland Gaul and beer from Egypt. Let's celebrate the Ides this month with tasty morsels of imported food and drink. The moon is especially bright now."

"Thank you." Brutus was unusually humble in the presence of Emperor Claudius. He had witnessed firsthand the brutality that Emperors are capable of administering.

"How is your court working, do you enjoy the privilege to sit in the memory of the Great Julius Caesar?"

Brutus was purposely brief today. "Yes." Brutus enjoyed his rare visits with the Emperor; they both seemed to savor the power they could exert over other people. Only Brutus was more personal than the Emperor. The terror he brought out in his prisoners, he saw firsthand in their eyes. "Your message was not specific, you requested my presence to discuss an urgent matter. Tell me, how is your Empire these days?" Brutus was trying to sense the real mood of the Emperor.

Brutus had been annoyed by the deficiencies in Rome over the last years—shortages of attendants and amenities at the baths. He had not enjoyed smoked boar meat from Gaul for some time. He was grateful the Emperor offered him some today. Fewer camels had been seen in Rome packing spices from India. Egyptian beer had disappeared from the tabernae he frequented. Brutus sensed not all was well. He was hoping the Emperor would address these deprivations.

"My friend, I would not normally tell the truth to such a question. I, the Emperor, can solve any problem like a god, Roman or Greek. However, I did ask for your presence to address some issues." Claudius stood up and paced about the room. Brutus flashed an agreeing smile. The Emperor continued, "The people are not working hard enough. You can see yourself the lack in Rome. The legions are not able to make their visits to all parts of the Empire as often as they should. Perhaps we conquered too much too quickly. The building of our towns in the occupied territories is consuming much time and resources. The roads connecting the Empire are being built at too slow a pace."

Brutus caught himself losing concentration on the Emperor. He would never have dreamed he would hear the Emperor openly doubt his past decisions. He was, after all, the descendant of the most conquering emperors in Roman history. He had inherited a most fortunate Empire and had just captured a jewel, Britannia, which two of his predecessors could not.

After each military conquest, there had always been an influx of new slaves from the conquered lands. Afterwards, more foreigners arrived via the roads built to accommodate swift movement of the armies. More foreigners had been showing up in his court of late. His courts were filled with petty thieves, especially from the docks during shipping season. They stole food from the tow-boats. Despite the free food available during festivals, which were happening almost daily, thievery was on the rise. Crime was rising, even with the entertainment provided at the Circus Maximus to keep the population occupied. He longed for more complex cases where he could condemn greater men to misery. Maybe even a son of God. But that didn't happen. He, like the Emperor, also needed his addiction to power satisfied.

"Do you agree, Brutus?"

Brutus was jolted from his self-absorbed thoughts; he had no idea what the Emperor was referring to. He knew all too well the fate of inattentive generals from past congresses. The Emperor's games always needed victims for the beasts to maul. He rubbed the rough stubble on his chin, looked carefully at the statue of Mars, the God of War, which stood beside the Emperor and responded. "Yes."

The Emperor stopped pacing and stared directly at Brutus. His face went into a scowl, his eyes flared, he seemed to suspend breathing; Brutus wondered what he had agreed to. Was he about to be hauled off and hurled over a cliff like the small pool boys? With a voice of disdain, the Emperor said, "So you think I should stop considering expanding my empire, take away my only source of joy and contentment. Remove the source for more slaves. Take away the delights of Gaul, Egypt and all places in between?"

Brutus knew he had to think quickly or not live to enjoy another sadistic hedonistic evening at the bath. In a low and humble voice he said, "Your highest, I would never suggest you abandon your plans for pleasures derived from the Empire. The land owned by Rome now is enormous. You successfully conquered Britannia, something even the great deified Julius Caesar was not able to do. Rome is the wealthiest city in the history of mankind. Over one million people enjoy the pleasures of living in Rome. You have surpassed the feats of all other emperors and nations. You exceeded the Greeks. You exceeded the Phoenicians and Carthaginians. You've demonstrated the power that is Rome."

Brutus knew he had to come up with something; his mind was racing as his tongue continued to flatter this suddenly crazy-eyed Emperor. Then an idea exploded into his head. His voice rose with excitement. "The citizens and subjects are always celebrating the activity of the sun as well as the moon and the stars. Their worship of the sky is an important part of their community. They are also constantly worshipping at the various temples of the gods. They feel these celebrations somehow empower them and will ease their suffering from life. They think that the celebrations will please the gods that control their lives. There is a festival for something almost every day. There seem to be more festivals than there are days of the week." He paused hoping for another idea to continue his story. "We need to change and divert this activity. We need them to take their festival time and put it into activities that will supply what we leaders and senators in Rome deserve."

The Emperor, now calmer, asked, "Are these activities widespread throughout the Empire?"

Brutus had no idea but answered, "Yes. Every region has a similar community of such activities, all a waste of good sunlight. As you know, when we conquer lands we allow their local customs to run alongside the new Roman laws. It has kept the social peace to a large extent. Palestine, of course, has always been a challenge."

Brutus knew that the conquering Roman legions allowed citizens of lands they captured to continue to practice their local customs. As long as there was compliance with the demands of Rome, their festivals were allowed to remain. The Jewish community had thrived alongside Roman expansion for many years. As long as taxes were collected and sent to Rome, the Emperors had allowed these communities to continue to honor their heritages. Yes, there had been revolts, but the Legions had acted swiftly to quell them. Brutality and torture were always displayed in public to discourage future rebellion. Individuals' outstretched arms were lashed to tree branches. Their legs were bound to tree trunks and nails were driven through their feet and hands. They were left to die. Rebellions against Rome were always addressed with force, harshness and dominance. The subjects must know the power of Rome and fear her torturous methods of punishment.

Brutus hoped this conversation would end soon, as he could no longer go on speaking confidently on a subject he knew nothing about. "Brutus, you have been a trusted colleague and now single-handedly have hit upon a solution to this problem. Yes, we must change the festival behavior of our subjects in order to serve the needs of you, me, and the senators of Rome. Go and devise a plan. You have until the Main Congress. You will present the orders there. I will immediately appoint you to my Inner Council.

"Also Brutus, examine the Cult of Caesar and see if you can reinforce it. I need a stronger hold on my power. As you know, some Senators are against my being leader. The Cult will gain support for me and future emperors who need protection from their enemies. We need a strong connection with the lower class masses of Rome, like Caesar was able to achieve. They were a formidable force during his funeral. They exercised their power as a group effectively. I and future emperors may need that mass protection in the event of a Senate uprising. To gain this support, we must reinforce the deep-felt belief that the Emperor is the Deity on earth, with the blessings of all the gods. The Star of Caesar declared it so." The Emperor finally sat down in a chair and focused his eyes on the floor near the base of the statue of Mars.

Brutus knew all too well what happened to the generals of the Inner Council when the Emperor bored of their advice. There was, as usual, a scheduled Emperor's Games the week after the Main Congress. Participants were always needed. Among them always were some from the Congress.

Those who displeased the Emperor were dispatched to the gallows of the Circus Maximus immediately to await their punishment. The mauling by wild beasts was always the fate of the worst offenders.

Not wishing to extend the conversation, Brutus remained silent. He waited for Claudius to speak. He was starting to regret his visit today. A small bead of nervous perspiration rolled down the center of his back under his toga. He hoped the dampness was not visible, as it might be interpreted as a sign of weakness. After what seemed like several minutes the Emperor finally spoke, "That is all, be swift in your thinking, Brutus." He motioned to his sentries. Emperor Claudius looked agitated as he stood up and turned his back to the Magistrate.

Brutus was escorted from the Palace by the guards. He wandered the streets, past the empty vendors of the Forum. At the first shrine to Cybele he found, he made an offering. Her protection may be needed as his contact with the Emperor increased. He would make a rare visit to his lararium that evening. He hoped the ancestors had not abandoned him as his offerings had been few. He would stop at the Temple to Vesta and buy some sacred bread. That should help immensely. Yes, he would also offer his best wine.

Brutus entered the bath. The attendants left quickly. He was alone. He cursed. He exited the bath. There was nothing for him here.

ROME –
A PRIVATE CHAMBER

Time spent with the Emperor always made Brutus uneasy. The threat of instant annihilation worried him. He now wanted to watch games of slaughter and see blood flow from prisoners he had sentenced in his court, or Gladiators. He didn't care where the blood came from.

However, there were no games today so he would have to create his own sinister excitement. He walked briskly to his private courtroom. He summoned his small contingent of guards and ordered they go to the docks by the river and find a newly-arrived fair maiden. He knew there were many foreigners arriving in Rome every day. One could be easily found. The maidens from the Eastern provinces were his favorites. His addiction to domination desperately needed to be satisfied.

The guards knew where to place the unsuspecting captive. The dark and isolated dungeon below the secluded courthouse did not give away its secrets. The young girl was forced through the solid wooden doors and down the stairs. She was surprisingly silent.

The victim was prepared, laid on her back and lashed to the wooden rails. Her nakedness was appealing, her soft olive skin intriguing. Honey from a vessel hanging from the low ceiling slowly dripped over her breasts. The sweetness would soon be tasted. A rope was placed around her neck.

The preparations completed, the guards departed.

Brutus entered the dim room. Black shadows danced across the bound body of the victim, shadows cast from two flickering oil lamps. He stood gazing at his conquest. He took great delight in savoring the dread that was building within her. His anticipation was swelling. Picking a fig from a plate of food, he applied a small drop of honey to it, kissed it, then placed it on her abdomen. He tasted the sweetness of her breasts. Drawing a small razor-sharp dagger from under his toga, he pierced the skin above her heart. He gasped at the sight of bright red blood as it flowed and mingled with the sweetness of the honey. The small trickle of crimson clinging to the curves of her body increased his frenzy even more. He placed a bronze chalice on the floor to collect the dripping blood. The taste of honey and blood mingling on her smooth flesh was tantalizing to his lips and tongue. Her sensuality consumed him. His desire was raging.

His attention shifted to her hips. His hands gripped each side tightly. The softness of her skin further inflamed his lust. He forced himself upon her. His eyes were riveted on the anguish of her face. His eyes met hers. To his dismay, he detected resignation; she seemed to accept her fate. This infuriated Brutus. He delighted in creating fear in others and relishing the fear he produced. His thrusts increased with his madness. When his explosion ripped throughout her body, he pulled the rope tightly. Her neck jerked into an awkward angle. Her body contorted abruptly. The fig on her abdomen fell to the floor. His domination was complete. He picked up the fig from the cold floor, retrieved the chalice, turned his back on the corpse and walked away. He adjusted his judicial toga and climbed the stairs back up to the streets of Rome.

As he walked along the familiar cobbled stone alleyways

he breathed deeply, filling his lungs with the cool air. He listened to the sound of his boots hitting the hard surface. With every step he felt more alive. He headed to the closest taberna, the one he favored after his conquests.

A half-full mug of beer and a vessel of wine were placed on his table. Brutus sat down. He placed his chalice on the table and added some wine to the blood. He took the fig from his hand and placed it beside the chalice. He gazed at these as symbols of the maiden, the fig her body and the chalice containing her blood. After a few moments he slowly placed the fig into his mouth, reliving the experience in his memory. He deliberately bit down with force into the soft texture of the fig, delighting in its sweetness. It represented his total conquest of the body of another human being. The wine and blood added to his victory over the life of another. The ritual confirmed for him the power he could wield over people. He was also reminded of the old rituals in front of the lararium where he offered wine and bread to his ancestors for protecting his home. His compulsion for domination satisfied, normalcy returned. He had forgotten about the Emperor. After savoring the wine, he meandered through the streets of Rome and returned to the bath to soak in the warm waters. This was the Rome that Brutus revered. She provided for all his needs.

Guards removed the lifeless body and took it to one of the many common burial pits outside the city walls. They covered their noses with cloth to block the stench of rotting human flesh. They tossed the blood and honey-soaked body of the eastern maiden into the pit. She was but one of all the poor and nameless people who had died on the streets of Rome that day. She would not be missed.

VILLAGE 42

When Matthos finished his morning meditation, Teacher sent him to the seashore. "Watch for the fishermen returning, they will need help today as the catch will be bigger than usual."

Half running and half dancing, Matthos hurried towards the sea. He loved to help pull in the nets. It made him feel older than he was. He enjoyed the coolness of the water dripping from the nets onto his arms. He delighted in the feel of the slippery skin of the fish as they were unloaded from the boats. He liked being a part of the celebration of a good morning's outing.

Matthos reminded Teacher of himself when he was young. He still marvelled at the flight of the seabirds and how the sparkling stars faded from the night sky. He felt the Creative Spirit stir his soul as he observed the heavens and all creatures on earth. It reaffirmed his decision to abandon his cultural traditions. He reflected briefly back to his time in Syria and India. He had learned so much about Greek thinking and Eastern philosophy, so different from his ancestral ways. It reaffirmed his conviction to follow his heart.

Teacher walked briskly to the hut of Peterus. When he arrived, the others also gathered. Jeshua shared, "My fellow guardians, while sleeping three moons past, my inner vision revealed a disturbing story. The soldiers were laughing more than usual, apparently celebrating something. Behind them, the library in Alexandria where I spent several years working and studying was on fire. No attempts were being made to save it. As a matter of point, the soldiers were ensuring that the entire structure would burn. It took three days for the destruction to be complete."

Jeshua was silent; all the elders looked at him. Some shared they too had had visions of fire while sleeping but did not have the memory of the teacher. They all wondered why a dream of such tragedy was being presented to them. The loss of all knowledge from Egyptian and Greek thought, plus the loss of all man's observations of the heavens, was unimaginable. The destruction of such priceless knowledge seemed senseless. It would be irreplaceable.

If the dreams were truly visionary, then steps must be taken now to preserve Truth by duplicating all the books containing the Lessons. The fire seemed to be many years away in a time of a different emperor. The elders were silent. Somehow they knew their world was about to change, but how? When?

There was nothing else to say.

ROME
BATH-HOUSE

Brutus soaked in the bath, alone. Although his ritual with the maiden had satisfied him for a time, he now felt something different. A strange feeling gripped him, an apprehension he couldn't figure out. Looking at the reflection of his face in the small pool of water beside the bath, he was startled at what he saw. The frightened eyes of the prisoners he condemned every day were glaring back at him. He cursed. Fear, for the first time in his life, had invaded his heart. He now wished he had not met with the Emperor.

He was alone, and when alone he spoke out loud. The sound of his voice echoing back to him from the hard granite walls excited him. Now was a time to speak with authority. Brutus shouted to the walls, "The Rome I knew as a young man has vanished. The plentiful delicacies of the Empire are now few. Bath attendants, if they are present, are too old to offer stimulating comforts. The Emperor himself is too selfish and secluded to completely notice the hardships and shortages that have fallen upon Rome."

Brutus felt exhausted; his thoughts focused only on the past. He had to devise a scheme for the Emperor to solve these problems. His whole life had been spent in pursuing pleasure and exercising domination over others, not looking toward the future. Now he would have to use his imagination to create something—a myth, a story, a forgotten legend, perhaps a new imaginary hero. He needed to find something that would appease and protect the Emperor and restore the Rome of his past.

Brutus had been a runner as a young man. He remembered the Emperor at the time, Augustus, gathering all the runners together for a celebration feast before they were sent off to expound on the wonders of Rome. They would be given gold and silver coins depicting the divinity of the Emperor which they distributed throughout the Empire. The establishment of this courier system by Augustus ensured communication within the Empire, something that previous rulers had not achieved. Heroic tales of the Emperor were the messages the runners would broadcast throughout their journeys. They would elaborate upon military victories and stress his divine roots. The rule of Augustus was born under the long-haired star that was his deified father, Julius Caesar. Since they were the messengers of Rome, runners were revered, almost like gods. They were given extra sandals, but most ran barefoot on the soft ground beside the stone roads. Extra delicacies and treasures of the Empire were always available for the runners. As they departed, the subjects of Rome would line the streets and cheer. The Emperor would kiss their hands as a blessing to ensure their safe return in three moons time.

Brutus had particularly liked the southeastern route through Greece, Palestine and on to Egypt. During shipping season, he would board a ship and disembark in Gaza or Alexandria. He had been a simple man, not interested in the Greek philosophy schools or the Hebrew settlements he passed while running through Palestine. He had often observed scholars of all nationalities travelling to study at the Museum in Alexandria in Egypt. Brutus had heard that all the knowledge of the known world was being translated to Greek at the library in the Museum. He was not interested. Rather, he enjoyed the outdoors; the feel of the wind brushing his skin as he ran excited him. The crisp cool morning air he inhaled deep into his lungs when he resumed his run each day invigorated him. He celebrated the movement of his body and the pleasures it provided him. He was aware of the gods of creation of Rome and had heard about Greek gods and goddesses such as Zeus, Hermes and Aphrodite. That was of little interest to him. Rome was his alma mater. Rome was the center of his civilization. Nothing else mattered.

Brutus was getting distracted with his thoughts of the past. He had always lived in the present, but now he had to think about the future. Now he needed a story, a myth, an idea, something so bizarre it would somehow shock the entire Empire into embracing change. Something that would return Rome to its former glory and resume the supply routes of food and delicacies. Hedonism must be restored. The Emperor needed security. Brutus took a deep breath and thought to himself, "This Emperor is at times stupid and selfish, unaware of his citizens and subjects. He belittles the runners, sending them off like annoying dogs." No wonder that the runners were not motivated to spread the virtues of Rome. Perhaps the local priests, Pharisees and teachers were starting to have more influence on the people of the Empire. Perhaps the Roman messengers were being ignored. Brutus longed for an emperor like Augustus.

He had an idea. He would enlist the runners to act as spies in the villages. They would feign lameness and stay a few days, listening to village conversations. They would report back to him the ideas and conversations of the villagers and how they spent their days. They would learn why the supply chain to Rome had dwindled. He would need time to hear from the runners, so first, he must convince the Emperor to change the Congress meeting. A strategy began to unfold.

Brutus glanced at his reflection in the water again, now pleased at what he saw. His eyes were dark, shallow and wide. The sinister look had returned. "Enough of the future," he thought to himself. He stepped out of the bath. "Off to the drying room, maybe an attendant is sleeping and needs to be awakened," Brutus said to the silent hard walls. No one answered. He cursed.

SUNRISE
VILLAGE 42

Matthos could barely see the small dark speck on the road in the low morning sun. It grew larger and larger. He realized it was a Roman runner, walking with a limp. He had been warned many times that the village must welcome the runners, so he alerted the elders. They prepared a resting place. Maria was summoned to administer medicinal aid. She prepared some healing tea.

Matthos, being curious, hid behind the fire bush and watched the runner. He was amazed to see him stand up, stretch his body and move his limbs, but when someone approached, suddenly he was unable to walk. Matthos found this very unusual.

The villagers went about their usual activities of fishing, maintaining the fire and drawing water from the well. They acted as if the runner wasn't there. When the runner asked for food and water, he was given it.

Jeshua had noticed that the runners from Rome had not been their usual exuberant selves lately. They had not been talking about the Emperor and Rome, nor had they carried coins bearing the image of the Son of God for some time. They said very little while they rested at the village. What they did say lacked passion. They looked tired and uninspired. After a few days, the lame runner left.

Teacher could tell something was amiss in Rome. The Emperor's court was not being celebrated in the usual zealous way. He had heard that Emperor Tiberius had been a recluse at his villa far from Rome prior to his death. Emperor Caligula could not unite the leaders and was assassinated after three short years as supreme leader. The Senate was restless and lacked direction. The enthusiastic runners during the reign of Augustus had all vanished. He gathered the elders together. "I feel we must accelerate our plan," he said. "The runners have no life, no spirit, and no passion. Who can blame them? We've heard little about the Emperor lately. He seems to have lost interest in the Roman provinces." Teacher paused, gathering his thoughts. All remained silent. Then he spoke. "Summon Matthos; it is time to expedite our work."

ROME
BRUTUS' CHAMBERS

The Congress opened half a moon cycle later than scheduled. The Emperor had actually liked the suggestion made by Brutus to delay the meeting. It allowed for more parades of the Emperor around Rome and more events at the Circus Maximus where he was seen and addressed. Brutus had grown to dislike Claudius more and more, especially for his disregard of runners. Brutus was making inroads in getting their trust. After all, he had been one of them.

Under the din of the Congress festivals, the reports from the returning runners bore a similar theme. The local teachers and priests were becoming more influential than Rome. All the villages throughout the Empire practiced similar activities and celebrations.

They had developed a sense of connection to a creative spirit through nature. The sun's yearly movements were watched and celebrated. They also observed the movement of the glittering stars and the cycles of the moon. This was why there were so many local festivals. They danced when the moon disappeared for three days and when it was a full small white sun in the dark night sky. They would sometimes gaze at the stars in the night sky, trancelike. Some claimed to see shapes of things in the sky, outlines of people or animals. Rituals were performed to connect with this supernatural spirit.

There was a village teacher in Palestine at Village 42 spreading the story that every person was a creation of some living force. A force that was only one God, not many gods as Romans and Greeks knew to be true. This God was unlike the Jewish God who is vengeful and beyond mankind. He and his followers believed that this Intelligence created everything. It resided not only everywhere in nature but also inside the heart of every mortal being. When each person realized this, his life was his own; he would not be controlled by others. He would not need religious leaders or emperors to tell him how to live. His power was his self-reliance. His sufferings were relieved. As well as this bizarre philosophy, there was also the usual appeasement of the gods as seen in Roman Temples.

Brutus was amazed by these stories. He recalled as a runner through Greece passing by the Socrates schools. He occasionally wondered how the Greeks lived their lives with so many gods to appease. Brutus emulated Zeus, who threw his thunderbolts at will. He felt close to Zeus. His thunderbolts of "guilty" were enormously pleasurable for him.

He needed to develop a program; there was not much time. The Congress had begun. All the Consuls were present. He convinced the Emperor to schedule him last on the agenda just before the final Worship of the Emperor ceremony. That way, if the Emperor liked his plan, he could claim to all present that it was his idea. The Emperor insisted Brutus sit next to him throughout the entire proceedings.

Brutus concluded that the constant celebrations and festivals encouraged by local teachers were the cause of the decline of imported delicacies into Rome. Participation of the Roman subjects in the festivals resulted in their neglecting the efforts required to supply Rome with the bounties it required. This must be changed. The needs of Rome and her leaders must be the focus of all activities.

Brutus was particularly concerned about the report from the runner spy who ran through Palestine. The small wayside hamlet, Village 42 on the seaside road, appeared to be more active than its small population would warrant. There was a group of twelve elders who seemed to be led by a reluctant teacher. He appeared not only to be a teacher but also a stonemason who worked with wood. Evidently, he had a temper. The runner had overheard an argument between him and the elders. It was about an inner sun God within every person. A God that, when realized, brings contentment and joy to all. The teacher was very vocal that no one member of the group would be a Messianic leader. The group's purpose was to help people discover their own inner sacred sun. He explained his teachings using metaphors and parables. They were meant to guide individuals to their inner sun. When a person was ready to discover it, the words would make sense. The group of twelve looked up to the teacher as their leader. Some people called him their Messiah. He strongly discouraged this, in fact was emphatic about it. He was not their savior. Rather, every man was his own messiah.

It was after this argument that the runner decided he had had enough of sitting. His legs were starting to go lame for real as a result of inactivity. He left after sundown so no one would follow. He found the argument very amusing. He thought about the gods of Rome, which comforted him on his journey home.

Brutus found this intriguing. There were no reports from other spies about dissension among other teachers and their elders. Yes, some regions resented the presence of the army legions and the towns they were building. But there were no major revolts across the Empire. Brutus wanted to know more. He felt something about this region might prove useful. Time was running out. However, he thought he had enough information to formulate a program to present to the Emperor and the Assembly.

But Brutus wanted more information about this teacher and why there was so much dissension in the group. This could be his answer to the troubles plaguing Rome. He knew a second lame runner arriving at the village would raise suspicion. He came up with an alternate plan to discover more about the happenings at Village 42. He summoned a new courier.

~

The young runner never liked to travel in darkness, especially when the moon hid for three nights. However, he must do as instructed by Brutus. As he approached Village 42, he veered toward the sea. He waded quietly into the still water, ensuring his clothing was completely soaked, then crawled under a boat and waited to be discovered. As instructed, when detected he would claim to have fallen overboard from a passing cargo ship.

ROME
THE SENATE

"My supreme Emperor, members of the Inner Council, colleagues from Gaul to Egypt, welcome to the last day of our State of the Empire Congress." Brutus enjoyed the attention of being the only speaker to be presenting today, much like being the justice in his court. He found his booming voice bouncing back to him invigorating. As agreed, if the Emperor liked what he was about to hear, he could claim all the credit.

Brutus continued … "The Empire is getting soft; goods and delicacies are not reaching Rome as they should. Our subjects are spending too much time with their festivals and feasts and traditions. This must change. Their activities should be focused on our needs, not theirs. Our soldiers' efforts are concentrated on building new towns. Their dedication is fierce and complete. However, they lack the resources to monitor all the subjects' activities, so it is up to us, the Congress, to devise a plan to solve our problems. We must have a program that serves Rome."

Brutus paused. His thoughts seemed somewhat fragmented. He looked around the huge hall. All were awaiting his next statement. "We will usher in a new doctrine of Rome, one based on our Emperor. He will be declared divine, God, just as Zeus in Greece. He will be deified while living, not upon his death. He will be worshipped at all prescribed festivals. He will be deemed to have power over prosperity and fertility. He only will issue land deeds and birthrights. All will worship him. His power will be mysterious. It will only be awarded through prescribed channels.

"We will work harder and with more diligence to remove from the streets of Rome those unnecessary aspects of daily life. Emperor Augustus started this cleansing, we will continue. All magicians, astrologers, members of foreign religions and anyone who expresses discontent with the decisions of the Senate shall be driven away. Nothing will detract the subjects from our mission. The Emperor is supreme."

Brutus paused again ... he thought his idea was not really much different from what the Emperor thought of himself right now. He continued, "We will create a new legion in our army dedicated to spreading the word of our new Emperor-God. More couriers will carry the message. All who wish health, salvation from their toils, or eternal life like the kings of Egypt—" ... Brutus caught himself; he should not have said that ... but after a pause said, "Yes, all who want to have eternal life, just as the pharaohs of Egypt, must accept the teachings of the Emperor. The local teachers must be silenced." Brutus felt he had said enough. As the applause subsided, he smiled at the Emperor and gracefully waved his arm, offering him the floor.

"My dear Brutus, you have articulated exactly what I asked of you."

Brutus saw a reflection of himself in the water that had spilled on the table. He couldn't tell which eyes looked back. He was concerned. The spy he had sent to Village 42 was overdue.

SUNRISE
VILLAGE 42

The morning sunrise shone brightly as it skipped across the gentle waves of the sea. The onshore breeze was cool and refreshing. Teacher had noticed that the overboard sailor appeared to be in no hurry to return to Rome or Egypt. He didn't say where he was from. He just sat, gazing out to sea. However, when Teacher walked about and spoke, he noticed the man was always nearby. He suspected the sailor was not familiar with the activity of the spice and incense merchants from Gaza or Alexandria, or even Rome.

Jeshua decided it was time to reveal more about the spiritual truths he had come to know. His sermons were now well attended. He was amazed and pleased at the people who listened intently to what he was saying. Even scholars travelling between Alexandria and other provinces would stop and ask about his teachings, the Lessons he had started sharing with Matthos all those years ago, the Lessons that were now hidden in the well, the Lessons that were now being duplicated as quickly as possible.

More people were gathering, more travellers lingering. Word about his new and radical message was spreading. The full moon had appeared in the previous night's sky. It was time for today's instruction. A short poem which expressed his Truths would be revealed today.

Teacher walked slowly up the road to the Mount of Olives, his chosen location for the sermons. He began, "From the priests of Egypt, the philosophers of Greece, and the teaching from the East, we have been blessed with much spiritual understanding. We must be thankful and filled with gratitude for their study. These practices are all recorded at the great Library of Alexandria in Egypt. I spent seven years there copying some of these treasures."

Jeshua went on to explain how those who had come before them had observed the wanderings of the stars, the sun and the moon as they travelled across the skies. They had contemplated the meaning of life and death within the context of their natural environment. From different cultures, they had uncovered similar ancient ways explaining how these creations of truth were expressed in nature. The natural world reflected back to every individual the characteristics of the divine spirit that resides within themselves. For example, the sun shines on all people regardless of social position, race or culture, just as the inner divine creative spirit is available to all regardless of social position, race or culture.

He explained how this spirit of creation could be accessed by each individual. It was not necessary to follow any social leader, such as their priests or the rulers of Rome, to find the joy that resides within their own hearts. He stated, "Every man, woman and child has the innate ability to contact their spiritual Father. Our judges, priests and emperors are not necessary for us to have a purposeful and peaceful life." Teacher knew not everyone would agree with him. When he spoke, he often saw the Pharisees in the crowd getting agitated. They disliked anyone suggesting their authority over the people of Judea was suspect or not necessary. They considered themselves the true carriers of spiritual messages as revealed through Moses. Their teachings must prevail. Peterus was alert.

Jeshua re-centered himself quietly among the gathered crowd. He told the people he was going to share with them a brief poem that would help them realize their inward divine selves and live a peaceful life. He called it the poem of Self- Realization. He began:

"Our Father."

He explained, "These two words refer to that Divine Creator, the giver of life, the one God who is the same for every nationality or culture. All mortals are a brotherhood looked upon by a compassionate Father, not a tyrant demanding appeasement and sacrifices. This is the true nature of mankind, individuals, and God and the bond between them. We are all One in the realm of Creative Spirit.

"Which art in Heaven, hallowed be thy name."

Jeshua explained, "The Divine Creative Spirit Father is the true giver of life, just as any loving family father is here in the earthly plane. Just as a physical father passes his qualities to his children, our basic mortal nature is also divine and hallowed or whole or healed. We all possess a sacred inner sun.

"Thy kingdom come, thy will be done on earth as it is in heaven."

He continued his dialogue, "The Divine Spirit is expressed through each and every one on earth. Attitudes that a person embraces within his mind and heart are expressed in the environment around his body. With the attributes of the compassionate Father held in your minds and hearts as you go about your daily affairs, you will attract success and happiness into your lives.

"Give us this day our daily bread.

"Only we can live our lives. No one can eat our bread for us; we are responsible for our own nourishment, both physical and spiritual. We need to live in the present and neither dwell on the past nor fret about the future. There is a continual expression of spirit which does not stop. It manifests at all times. It is eternal.

"And forgive us our debts as we forgive our debtors.

"This line refers to the nature of the relationship between all peoples. The way we behave toward others will be the way others respond to us. We will be judged as we judge others. We reap what we sow. The harvest reflects the seed that was planted, just as a farmer can only harvest grapes from the grape seeds he plants. He cannot harvest grain from those grape seeds. Respect from other people is not gained by deceitful behavior towards others. It is earned by being respectful towards others. That is the way of Creative Spirit. An attitude of forgiveness is one of the most powerful inner tools for individual health and happiness. This attitude also forces one to live in the present.

"Lead us not into temptation, but deliver us from evil."

Further understanding was shared. "The more aware you become of this Divine Intelligent Spirit, the greater is your responsibility to express it and acknowledge the Source. These words caution followers not to allow their attitude to shift away from the Truth, not to allow self-importance to creep into their consciousness. Affirm that spirit is the Source of all things. As we experience the Truth, we need to humbly take responsibility for our lives.

"For thine is the kingdom, power and glory forever.

"This phrase reiterates the source of real truth; there is one compassionate, omnipresent God, creator of all, and a spark of that spirit resides within each person on earth, like a spirit that dances as a sunray upon the waters of a celestial sea. It is eternal.

"Om.

"This word from the East is always heard by the Creator and concludes the Poem of Self-Realization. Expression of truth and kindness is the way, the Tao of life. As individuals realize their divinity, it will flow as compassion from their heart towards others and will free them of their illnesses and shortcomings."

Jeshua paused for few minutes; he wanted them to absorb what he had just said. He then repeated the poem slowly without explanation, so they could hear it again in its entirety. He explained how to use the poem. "Every day, find a peaceful place to sit quietly. Close your eyes and relax your body and mind. Repeat these lines one by one. Pause after each line, and let your mind and inner sun grasp the words. Your mind will become more aware of your spirit each time you do this. Do not rush through these words. They will guide you to more awareness of your sacred self. You will soon perceive that you are the master of your own soul. You need no one to show you your way. Neither me, nor the leaders of our culture, nor the representatives of Rome are required for you to connect with your Fatherly spirit. No doctrine or system of rules is required for attunement to the divine."

Teacher explained that by repeating these words with a desire to understand and apply the Lesson of Divine Creation, their souls would eventually understand and rise above the earthly plane and its sufferings. There was nothing to fear. They would gain true personal understanding of their creation. They would be liberated from the denseness of their bodies. They would express their compassionate divine souls and see the same in all their fellow men.

Jeshua paused, closed his eyes for a few moments and continued. "Our priests tell us God is vengeful and must be feared. This is not true. God is compassion.

Once discovered, however, the Spirit of Creation must be respected. If lack of respect develops and vanity creeps into your consciousness, then troubles will come upon you. As a dam holding water that has no outlet to dispense it to nourish the fields, the pressure of Spirit can destroy. Self-serving attitudes will bring down the misguided person. The destruction is self-induced."

He continued, "The actions and words of the emperors and the Pharisees are not wise actions and words, they only divide cultures. They see all men as puppets to be manipulated and held in servitude to them. They are not of the Divine Will. The domains of the emperors and Pharisees will eventually fall and collapse and Truth will rise for all. The true purpose of Creation is to unify all under a tree of understanding and expressed compassion."

He paused and looked out over the crowd. His intention was not to annoy the judges of his culture. He must, however, be true to his soul, his Angel, and expose the false beliefs. He summarized his sermon with one last idea. "Learn to love your neighbor as yourself. When you apply these truths in your life you are being compassionate towards yourself. Express this love for those around you."

He noticed something moving up the road. It was the sailor running north towards Rome. He knew the man was not who he pretended to be. Peterus smiled at him. All was well.

ROME
BRUTUS' VILLA

Brutus was sitting in his rooftop garden basking in the morning sun. With the shipping season now open, he was again enjoying some rare delicacies from the Empire. Figs, olives, cheeses, smoked boar, North African tea, and pickled fish had been served by his slaves. He was reminded, albeit briefly, of how Rome used to be.

"Where is that runner?" Brutus thought to himself. He had been expecting the lost sailor for some time. Perhaps he had been wounded; possibly he had drowned when he approached the village. "My plan was not that dangerous," he thought to himself.

Then, off in the distance, he could see the figure, each stride as purposeful as the previous. His legs were moving on their own momentum. Exhaustion was starting to take hold of every fiber of his body. He remembered his own returns to Rome as a courier from Palestine. The gait of a spent runner was familiar to him. He recalled breathing in the smells and hearing the sounds of the city after being away for so long. He remembered how proud he had felt to be a citizen of the Empire. He had carried that pride with him then and today, even when the Empire appeared to be weakening. He hoped the runner would have some information he could use to change the fate of Rome. He needed to restore her brilliance. He must restore the Emperor to his rightful place as ruler of the world, provider for all.

The young runner narrowed his eyes; he could see the silhouette of Brutus standing on his rooftop. He slowed his pace. Fatigue was starting to overwhelm his entire body. He had stopped very little after leaving the teacher's sermon.

Brutus descended from the roof and rushed past the neglected lararium beside the entry to his villa. He didn't need to appease his ancestors to find a solution to his dilemma. He went to the street and stood to greet the runner. "Welcome home," was all Brutus said. He guided the physically spent man to the hearth and dismissed his slaves. Turning to the runner he said, "Have some nourishment and drink." He motioned towards the numerous delicacies spread out on the table. The young man looked at the food as if it were a feast. Village 42 was not as plentiful as anything in Rome. He sat at the table and savored the aroma and flavors of smoked boar, figs, pickled fish and Egyptian beer.

Brutus waited with uncharacteristic patience for the runner to finish. He remained standing beside the window. The sunbeams were lighting the food in a spectacular way. Brutus thought for a moment the gods must be smiling upon him. When the runner had eaten his fill, Brutus was brief with his words. "Meet me at the bath this evening." The runner left to rest.

Brutus was very pleased the courier had returned. He must give thanks. He carried some bread and wine to his neglected altar. He poured some wine into the ground and placed bread over the sacred flame. He covered his head with his toga and placed his hand over his heart. He touched the cool marble of his lararium. He prayed to Jupiter. He pondered upon the traditions of Rome.

ROME
BATH HOUSE

The bath was empty when Brutus arrived. No attendants were present. He was growing accustomed to the lack of services these days. He cursed as he remembered better times.

He spotted the runner at the end of the drying room. The two men sat. The courier started, "The teacher's name is Jeshua Christus. He tells of a strange God. A God that is loving, not vengeful like the Hebrew God, or contemptuous like the Greek gods. A single God." Brutus really wasn't interested in all this god talk. He was only interested in returning Rome to her glory and power as well as protecting the Emperor.

The runner continued, "This Jeshua teacher is not liked by the rulers of Palestine. He preaches independence of any leadership, dogma and ritual. Follow your own inner spirit and determine your own path is his message." Brutus thought he could take advantage of the hostility between Jeshua and the local leaders. He would find a way, but not today. He had heard all he wished, or thought he needed. He thanked the runner for his observations. They would be exceedingly useful, he was told. Praising the man for his service to the Emperor and the Roman Empire, he dismissed him from the bath.

He turned his attention to the festivals celebrated throughout the Empire. If he could find some way to channel some of these celebrations to Rome's benefit, he could create a program of change. This change must inspire all to work for Rome, supplying her with food, drink and entertainment.

Brutus left the bath. He stopped at the taberna near his villa. He ordered some wine and noticed an attractive server. He was formulating a plan in his mind. Sometimes he would walk among the subjects of Rome for inspiration, but not tonight. He finished his chalice of wine, took his turn with the server and returned to his villa. He stopped at his lararium. Another acknowledgement to the gods couldn't hurt.

The next day he realized that the runners could be a wealth of information. He called them to his chamber. As the chief of the Roman justice system, he had some power to give instructions not sanctioned by the Emperor. As a new member of the Inner Council, he was anxious to make his mark. He instructed the runners to return to their regions at once. They were to gather information about all the non-Roman festivals that were being celebrated and observed throughout the Empire. They would all meet back in his chamber before the next Emperor Games. He bid them all a fond farewell and a speedy return.

Neil Anthes

ROME
BRUTUS' VILLA
51 A.D.

Word from the new runner just returned from Palestine was not what Brutus had expected. The teacher at Village 42 had suddenly died. His teachings had stopped. Many were deeply saddened and shocked. However, the elders of the village were planning to continue the Lessons at each full moon.

Brutus seized upon an idea to help formulate the changes required to the festivals celebrated by all of Rome. He could take advantage of the uncertainty the teacher's death had caused among his followers.

Unknown to Brutus, the Pharisees in Palestine and priests at the Temple of Jerusalem were also very happy and relieved concerning the teacher's death. The uneducated at the Temple were claiming Jeshua was their Messiah. This was extremely disturbing to the traditionalists of the Hebrew people.

The priests and scribes now worked to eradicate Jeshua's words, which had been spread now for twenty years. They would be discounted. The Lessons would be excluded from the historical vaults of writing secretly being hidden in the caves near the Salty Sea. Time would eventually destroy all evidence of the teachings. Their mission was now to revive the intensity of the activities at the Temple and remove Jeshua's influence on their tribe.

VILLAGE 42

Sitting under the olive tree in the shade, Maria reflected upon her time with Jeshua. Her thoughts roamed back to the early times in Alexandria. She recalled her favorite time of year when the summer heat had broken. It now all seemed like a dream to her. In a moment, she was transported back almost thirty years. A gentle smile grew across her face as her mind drifted.

She remembered the evening she had met Jeshua. He was sitting alone on a bench in the garden. He had smiled as she walked by and asked her to sit beside him. She had noticed him before, a small man with bright brown eyes and clear olive skin. His face was rugged. He had a calmness and gentleness about him that intrigued her. She sat beside him.

"Maria, are you well? Is the heat too much for you?" Peterus said, approaching.

"I was recalling the third time Jeshua and I travelled to Upper Egypt. I am quite fine; closing my eyes brings the memories back easier. I will join the others soon." She felt the hard bark of the tree on her back. It reminded her of the floor of the cave where she and Jeshua had slept that evening. Transported back to Egypt, she could see the rising sun reflecting off the canyon wall and feel the cave warming up. She and Jeshua rose from their sleep and felt the cool night air being chased away by the sun's beautiful rays. They marvelled at the new day. They always sat cross-legged towards the morning sun for a few moments and meditated. Once completed, they enjoyed figs and dried fish. The beer was refreshing that morning, a local brew from the barley fields their boat had passed the day before.

Jeshua would always bring a book with him. She never knew which one. They would walk to the edge of the red land and stroll among the low canyons. He would find a cool sheltered spot and read the book aloud. She heard the works of Plato, the Buddha, more writings from Cicero, as well as many other philosophers. The common thread in all the books was that mankind had a divine soul. Yes, a spirit that was a spark of creation itself. We could access this power within ourselves during our lifetime here on earth. Life was a continuum; there was no death for the soul, the inner sun, the personal spirit, only many journeys. He would reflect on how the customs of our people denied this existence within each and every one. The importance of tradition and slavish adherence to religious law actually smothered individual access to our divinity. Life was not about appeasing any god—Greek, Roman, Egyptian or Hebrew.

It was time for Jeshua to reveal his surprise. The book he had brought for this visit was about ancient Egyptian religion. He read aloud about the beliefs of the ancient Egyptians. The sun rising every morning showed how it overcame its own death from the prior evening. Each night it entered the underworld and traveled through it over the entire night, then celebrated its victory each morning. The ancient Egyptians believed they too would conquer their own death, just like the sun.

Jeshua went on to explain the symbol of the river. "Each year the Nile floods, symbolizing the cycle of life. After the harvest the black land is baked dry by the hot sun and cracks. Nothing grows. Even the crocodiles have problems staying alive. Then the flood comes every year and brings life back to the fragile lands. The gazelles return, hippopotamus thrive, jackals and snakes return. All compete with the farmers for the life the river gives. This was also considered a sign that people would conquer their own death, just as the regenerating waters of the Nile returned life to the soil." The lotus flower that closes in the evening only to open again to the morning sun was considered another omen that mankind could conquer his own death.

As this part of Egypt was protected by the heat of the desert of the red land, no enemy could travel across the land and attack this area. As a result, the ancient Egyptians had a sense of security not enjoyed by other areas of the Mediterranean. Other countries could be easily invaded by neighbouring armies. As a result of this natural geographic protection, the Egyptians were free to develop their civilization with little disturbance from outside cultures. After all, it had only been about fifty years since Egypt became a Roman province.

Conquering death became a preoccupation of the Egyptians. They believed the afterlife would be the same as this life. The dead would need food, clothing, servants, furniture, even boats. Therefore, tombs were filled with these items. The more wealthy the person, the more would be required for the afterlife. Statues of servants and the deceased were placed in the tomb. During the post-death ceremony called "the opening of the mouth", it was believed that the priests would bring all the items to life that were accompanying the deceased in the grave. They all would live on in the earth, the underworld.

The east side of the Nile represented new beginnings, because the sun celebrated victory over its own death each morning by rising in the east. All burials were done west of the Nile, where the sun met his death each day sinking into the darkness of the night horizon.

The Pharaohs were considered sons of the great sun god Re; therefore, they owned all of the land in Egypt that the sun casts its rays upon. They built their tombs on the west side of the river. Rock was quarried and floated downstream on barges to the burial sites. Precious stones from the red land were used for all entombing rituals. The wood used for construction of the tombs was imported from the Eastern Mediterranean and transported by boats upriver. This trade of wood for quarried rock and precious stones thrived for centuries. The Romans used Egyptian granite for construction of their temples. Egypt also exported papyri to the world. All this was made possible by the river.

Maria found history interesting and enjoyed listening to Jeshua. He was a natural teacher. He knew how to tell stories that reflected his personal understanding of life. She could see he wanted to share what he knew. Deep down, however, she knew his knowledge, especially about discovering your own inner divine sun, would not be accepted or tolerated by the Roman consuls or even their own people.

She reflected on the fact that Jeshua was a mentally strong man, devoted to his own inner spirit. His daily activity reflected the wisdom he had acquired from his time working the spice trade routes and studying in India. He sat quietly facing the rising sun every morning, eyes closed. He held no resentment about the ignorance of Truth shown by the leaders of both Rome and the Temple in Jerusalem. He lived his life as a master of understanding. He wished no attention to be on himself. He said that all people, when aware of their power, had the ability to express the Creator if they chose to. Maria knew that Jeshua would eventually become a Teacher of Truth.

She thought how very content she had been with her life; her spirit was free. Jeshua would be missed but would live on within her heart. She opened her eyes and appreciated the natural beauty of the Eastern Mediterranean. She rose from her resting place and joined the others who had gathered in Jeshua's honor.

Matthos sat in the small cave, the place where he had heard his first Lesson from Jeshua. It was cool, protecting him from the harsh heat of the summer sun. He wanted to be alone for a few moments, distant from the mourners. He reflected on Jeshua.

Teacher had been vibrant and healthy all his life. He was dedicated to Maria's healing ways. He'd taken ill after last week's discourse and had difficulty breathing. Maria thought it was simply dust in the air from the passing sand storm and administered a mixed tea to calm him. He retired earlier than usual and died in his sleep without a sound.

The last sermon had been well attended; people had travelled from Greece and Syria to hear his words. Yes, the soldiers were watching and the Jewish leaders disliked him immensely; however, he had appeared content and healthy.

Matthos pondered more upon the life of his teacher and uncle. He had stayed away from the Temple of Jerusalem after he started his public teachings. His temper flared there. His temper would also rise when the elders talked of him as their leader. He was always quick to deny this assertion. He was forceful about denying his role as a leader and insisted he be considered only a teacher.

When questioned by the elders or anyone about how they should live their lives, he would always put the question back to the person asking it. It was his way of showing them that the answers they sought always lay within themselves. Seeking results from an outside source was not the effective way. He always referred to how each person was responsible for himself and should accept no leader over him, especially not him as a teacher. He suggested rejecting cultural authority from this perspective, but not disturbing the general social peace of the day. Jeshua often said that when one finds his inner sun god, he would also see it within others. Teacher had been wise. He would be missed by all. Matthos rose and joined the other mourners in the village.

Three days after the funeral, Maria and the elders sat under the olive tree in a circle. Peterus suggested they just sit quietly and remember their departed friend. He reminded the elders that no one is greater than another when sitting in a circle. This had been one of Teacher's constant reminders. With their eyes closed, they shared their common grief and celebrated the oneness of their spirit.

It was Maria who first stirred. She seemed to have heard a message from Jeshua, yet he was dead. Then Peterus received a message, then James, then Matthos, then Thomas. It appeared that the spirit of Jeshua was speaking from beyond the grave. The elders were amazed. Everyone grew very calm and relaxed. They now realized their beloved Teacher continued to exist beyond the body. His teachings had been verified. Spirit was eternal, no one was a follower; everyone was his own Messiah. Everyone had the same spirit within, regardless of nationality, race or social position. They now understood what Teacher had been telling them. They all stood in awe.

After a few more days, the mourners dispersed. The village was quiet. Despite their grief, peacefulness fell over everyone. Matthos knew he now had to follow Jeshua's last instructions. He conferred with his father James, who agreed it was time to follow his brother's request. If word was spreading about the teacher who had done the impossible, spoken to his wife and elders three days after his death, Rome would become agitated. They waited until late afternoon. They went to the well, gathered thirteen leather-bound codices, placed them in a large earthen jar and sealed it with a bowl over the mouth. They placed other documents in hiding spots inside the cave near the village. These would be attended to upon their return. They hurriedly started the journey to Upper Egypt, the jar hidden among bales in the donkey cart.

ROME

Brutus was getting bored. Reports from the runners about feasting and praising the movements of the sun and stars were not what he had hoped for. However, the situation at Village 42 presented an advantageous opportunity. For now, he had made progress in formulating an agenda for the required changes to Roman public life. He was considering the creation of a new festival or devising a new organization, something that would appeal to everyone. He would use the military, if necessary, to implement his plan.

Although of little interest to him, Brutus was aware that the gods controlled the lives of every Roman citizen and subject. He did not participate in all the festivals and worshipping. He did not enjoy going to the temples to witness the sacrificing of animals to each and every god. Hardly an animal lover—he enjoyed seeing the blood flow—it just took far too long to roast the meat and serve it to the people. They were mostly the poor and unemployed, the type he saw in his court most days. However, he did celebrate the festival to Jupiter, supreme ruler of the sky, and the festival to Mars, the God of war. He found Saturnalia entertaining, but felt it ran far too long. Neglecting the courts and all business for a week was not judicious.

He neither argued nor agreed with the senators when Emperor Augustus was declared divine and given god status. He had been dead for thirty-seven years. He had been acknowledged as a son of a god for over sixty years.

One more god seemed fine to him.

Brutus now ignored the lararium in his home; he considered spending any moments in front of that altar a waste of time. He was aware that others, even his slaves, worshipped at it every day. Most Romans first spent time at their lararium before leaving their homes for the day. It was necessary to honor the dead and appease their chosen god. Brutus felt and experienced his own power in his court every day. He did not need to summon the gods. He believed that if the gods controlled his life, just let them do it. He enjoyed the barbaric and bloodthirsty side of Roman life. He always arrived early at the Circus Maximus when the public games, Ludi Romani, were held. The aromas of roasting pigs and other foods were tantalizing. He tasted the preparations of the shop keepers who worked to provide for the two hundred and fifty thousand people who would attend the games. Always free to everyone, the games now extended over several days. That way, the poor and unemployed were kept occupied and fed. After each military conquest, the population of Rome grew in numbers and diversification as more unskilled people and slaves made Rome their home. This was the new reality.

Brutus admitted he derived pleasure from the games. He especially savored the gladiators' fights. These hired men slowly hacking each other to near death with swords and clubs, inflicting bloody wounds, was his type of entertainment. When the crowd decided that the vanquished gladiator should die at the hands of the victor, Brutus was enlivened. The wild beast hunt was another of his favorites. The gladiators would wrestle with hungry beasts. The beasts always won. Public executions were something he never missed. A wild creature tearing apart a hopeless prisoner tied to a post was an event he found most rewarding. It reminded him of his power over others in his court. It stirred his frenzy. He enjoyed the bloodthirsty side of Rome. He always cheered lustfully with the crowd when a racing chariot at Circus Maximus lost its driver and he was trampled to death by the other horses and competitors. Sadism, dominance and death were Brutus' entertainment. He also had the pleasures of his private hidden dungeon to satisfy his occasional need for total dominance.

Brutus knew the rulers of Rome encouraged these festivals to appease the unemployed and the poor. Free food and public games several times a month helped to keep social unrest to a minimum. It was a necessary activity to keep the peace. He felt he was contributing to the public cause, as the prisoners he declared guilty were often used in the wild beast bloodbath.

His mind came back to his current dilemma; the future of Rome depended on his insight. He had heard all the runners reporting the same strange stories. Teachers and priestesses throughout the Empire were talking about nature and creation and the worship of the sun. Then there was the fantasy about a single compassionate God. What could be more bizarre? Everyone knew there were many gods, each controlling an aspect of mortal life. How could he get the subjects attending all the foreign festivals to listen to something different? How could he get those celebrating just the Roman festivals to also change? How could he divert their attention to the needs of the elite? How could he redirect their enthusiasm? Brutus concluded there was only one way to divert and change the activities of the masses. Whispering aloud, he concluded, "Rome needs a new state religion."

For this project to work, Brutus concluded, all traces of spiritual truth must be destroyed. When he had been a runner for Emperor Augustus, he had passed many Socrates schools in Greece. These schools must be closed and all collections of parchment, tablets and papyrus destroyed. Nothing in written form could remain.

The libraries at the Museum of Alexandria would have to be destroyed as well. With the Emperor's approval, a plan would be hatched. It must appear to be an accident. Brutus got this idea from the tragic time when Julius Caesar was in Alexandria. His ships had caught fire in the harbor and threatened to set fire to the city. Luckily, disaster had been averted. Fire would again be set to the ships but this time the flames would be allowed to spread. The ships would drift towards the city and the libraries would be destroyed. The army consul may have to be part of the plan. No one else except Brutus and the Emperor would know the reasons behind the destruction.

Brutus knew Rome had to appear friendly to the Greek schools and librarians of Alexandria. Burning the libraries may force other materials in other locations throughout the Empire into hiding places that may be difficult to locate. He sensed the need to assemble a hidden library to store any confiscated material. There was a large secret room deep beneath the chambers of his courtroom that would serve the purpose. Speaking aloud to himself, he said, "Perhaps this would be a more acceptable and less noticeable way to eliminate all traces of Truth. The future will require a re-sorting of accepted knowledge. The books may be useful in a different age."

Brutus sent the order via his fastest runner to the local soldiers stationed in Palestine. They must immediately go to Village 42. They must stop any attempts to continue the teachings of Jeshua. They must search the area for any books containing his teachings. If any were found, they were to be confiscated and sent to him immediately. His scheme was directed specifically at the teachings of Jeshua Christus.

PALESTINE

The sentries immediately marched to the village. A few papyri and bound codices were found in a cave near the huts. They were gathered up and prepared for transport. These writings were among the first of many books that Brutus would hide beneath the Justice Hall of Rome. The soldiers arrested and enslaved the elders and the few able-bodied men left in the village. All were sent to Rome.

As the soldiers were leaving Village 42, a donkey cart laden with straw bales, papyri and earthen jars stopped for water. When the driver was finished, the soldiers destroyed the well, the huts, the boats and the entire village.

The donkey cart headed east across the sands of the desert. Arriving in Jerusalem, the driver unloaded the papyri at the Temple. They were placed in earthen jars which were then sealed and reloaded onto the cart. The driver continued on his journey. He knew he had to go further than a day's travel beyond the last road. When he reached the mountains east of Jerusalem, he headed south towards the Salty Sea. He searched for a large cave complex on the west side overlooking the waters. One was located with many passageways carved out of the rock. It would serve well for the purposeful preservation of the contents of the jars.

The earthen jars were placed in the first opening and the entrance to the cave was sealed. The traveller looked back to the southeast and watched the sunrays dance off the waters of the Salty Sea in the distance. He took a bearing to remember where the entrance could be found for the next visit. After the riots instigated by the Roman soldiers at the last Passover, the High Priest, fearing Rome may one day attack the Temple of Jerusalem and destroy their scared writings, had ordered the duplication of all chapters of the Torah and other temple writings. The copies were to be hidden in the rock cave complex in the desert. This was the first of many books to be hidden and protected.

EGYPT

Matthos and James were tired, hungry and thirsty. They looked forward to returning to the village and resting in their own huts. Sleeping in road ditches was not comfortable. Every time a runner or legion of soldiers approached, they would venture into the desert and hide.

The journey to the outer edge of Egypt had taken longer than anticipated. However, that was Teacher's wish. They had traveled to Upper Egypt by freight boat up the Nile to where the river takes a big bend and disembarked there. Heading west as directed, the caves and cliffs were exactly where Teacher had said. In the red land, things would stay preserved for many years. The west side of the Nile would be least visited as it represented the death of the sun. The books would stand a better chance of remaining hidden there than on the east side. Teacher did not know how long it might be before Rome would again be friendly to the people of Palestine. Matthos had been instructed never to reveal the location where he hid the jar … at the base of the Jabal al-Tarif cliff near Chenoboskion. The task completed, they pushed hard to get back to the village.

VILLAGE 42

Matthos and James were not prepared for what they saw. Their huts had been destroyed, the well filled with debris and all the fishing boats were gone. The elders and other neighbours had disappeared. Matthos' initial reaction was to hate the soldiers, then he remembered Teacher's lessons. He was responsible for his own life, he was self-reliant. The soldiers can create difficulties, yes, but they were ignorant of their own power. They merely followed the direction of a corrupt leader. Matthos decided to look upon them with compassion, for they were the ones who had fear and hatred in their hearts. He rushed to the cave where he had hidden the other scrolls and codices. Everything was gone.

Matthos sat dejected under the olive tree. He reflected on the many hours he had spent with Jeshua and the hours he, Thomas and James had recorded the Lessons in the now empty cave. Village 42 had vanished. There was nothing remaining. It was time to move on, somewhere far away—perhaps Italy. His father James decided to travel to Galilee as Maria would be there at her father's home. He was, after all, her brother-in-law. He would help with her healing practice. He knew where medicinal plants could be found throughout the deserts. Father and son bade a fond farewell.

Matthos headed south back towards Egypt, this time with nothing but a small satchel and some coins for the road tolls. He arrived at the seaport Gaza and went to the docks. Thankfully, a few ships were still there. The shipping season was about to end as winter approached. He quickly found work and passage to Rome on a spice boat. The cloves and black pepper were to be his companions for the sea voyage.

When he arrived at the seaport of Ostia at the mouth of the Tiber River, he decided to find a cart to Rome rather than a river tow boat. The boats were slow as the oxen pulling them from the shore with attached ropes often went lame. The boat operators were not kind to their beasts of burden.

The cart bumped and heaved along the stone road into Rome, tossing everything about, including Matthos. Mausoleums for those who could afford to bury their dead were scattered along the sides of the road. The baker's shrine in the shape of a huge loaf of bread was the most unusual he had ever seen. The stench from the open burial pits beside the road leading to the city was almost overwhelming at times He detected the smell of burning incense, frankincense and myrrh used to mask the odours. The aromas of the spices in the cart also helped.

When he finally arrived in the city he was greeted by a menagerie of sounds, sights and smells. Everything was beyond his imagination. He could not imagine where the hundreds of thousands of people lived throughout Rome. The cart took him straight to the Forum. The temples were massive, the crowds daunting and the noise distracting. It was all overwhelming for a young man from a small village in Palestine.

Suddenly, he thought he saw Peterus from his village, but that would be impossible. Peterus loathed the Romans with their aggressive and intruding behavior. Rome was a place of blood, domination and greed, everything Peterus disliked about the world. He was even starting to question why he himself had travelled to Rome.

Peterus could not believe his eyes; Matthos was in Rome! He must not show any recognition or Matthos would be arrested by his guard. Peterus looked away, then glanced over his shoulder to make sure it truly was Matthos in the distance.

Matthos decided he must be seeing things. He needed food and sleep. He searched the unfriendly streets of Rome for both. He found a resting place beside Vesta's Temple in the Forum. Everyone there was friendly towards him. As he rested, his heart sank as he recalled the destroyed village and the empty cave. His own writings of Teacher's lessons from the Mount of Olives he had left to be retrieved on his return were gone. He wondered about the fate of the books that had been in the cave. Perhaps they had been burned in a cooking fire by soldiers. If he could find writing materials in Rome, he vowed he would copy what he remembered. Sleep mercifully overtook his hunger. A strange and visionary dream emerged.

ROME
BRUTUS' VILLA

Brutus could only read Latin, not Greek or Hebrew, or whatever it was he was looking at. The books from Village 42 had arrived. He addressed the captured elders from the village and assigned them to his secret library. His guards escorted the elders, now slaves, to their meagre quarters.

Brutus sat alone. He was getting frustrated. His project was stalled. He was growing weary. He missed his courtroom where he could create fear and exert total control over others. His addiction was not being satisfied. He needed his dungeon occupied.

Brutus was indeed stumped. The ideas were not flowing. How could he get his new public religion of Rome organized so all subjects and citizens would find it acceptable? The constant celebration of festivals must stop. People must focus on what Rome needed. He never liked how, after each new conquest of a country by the generals and their legions, the defeated were allowed to continue their local celebrations with observance of the Roman festivals imposed on them. Then, a few years later, it seemed the festivals of the conquered were being celebrated somewhere in Rome. He disliked this casual acceptance of other cultures' historical feasts. The conquered should forfeit all to Rome. Since Saturnalia was the most popular of all festivals and appeared to be celebrated by almost all Romans, Brutus decided his new religion could be established at that time of year and ultimately replace Saturnalia.

His mind now moved to past historical heroes from Greece and Rome. Eventually they had been declared a god or a son of a god. Emperor Augustus was declared a god after his death. That Macedonian, Alexander the Great, was declared divine by Egyptian priests. It gave credibility to the people of the region if their new ruler was divine. It was believed that the Egyptian Pharaohs were all divine gods and that all their offspring inherited that trait. When a dynasty fell, the heirs were declared divine by the priests to keep the peace. In Alexander's case, his military genius was considered of divine origin. Who else but a god could conquer so much land?

Brutus knew all people believed that the gods adored mortal women. The gods visited favored women to pass their divinity on to the human race. After all, Silvia, the wife of Septimus Marcellus, had borne a child by the God Mars.

Brutus recalled several entertaining plays he had seen where foolish women were portrayed as giving themselves up to the embraces of corrupt priests, thinking they were being seduced by a god. This was common knowledge; the gods occasionally interacted with mortals. Hercules was the son of Zeus!

Two thousand years ago, the virgin Egyptian Queen Mut-em-ua gave birth to Pharaoh Amenophis III. He built the temple at Luxor. The God King Kneph impregnated her by holding the symbol of life, a cross, to her mouth. The gods had been making direct contact with mankind since the beginning of time.

The idea of divine intervention into the affairs of man gave credibility to new ideas, new leaders and new religions.

The masses seemed to be calmed by the reassurance that the gods were involved directly in their lives by displaying their power and pleasure upon their chosen mortal ones from time to time. Brutus decided his hero in this new Roman religion would definitely be a son of God. Why not pretend something happened somewhere in the Empire that could be used to start this religion, something involving a son of God. After all, not every single thing worshiped across the Empire could be known to the officials in Italy. It would have to be something fictitious, something so remotely removed from reality that people might believe it. He picked up one of the scrolls the soldiers had brought from Village 42. He wished he could fully understand Hebrew. Somehow he felt this document of Jeshua's teachings could be useful.

He abruptly summoned the slaves from his hidden library and demanded they interpret the writings of the scroll. They claimed to understand very little. Yet among them, Brutus kept hearing a name mentioned. The name was Matthos. "Who is this Matthos, and where is he?" Brutus demanded.

"He was the village scribe. The last time we saw him he was travelling to Egypt," Peterus replied. "We have no idea what his intentions were once he arrived. He may have stayed at the Museum as he was very interested in the books housed there."

Getting no useful information, Brutus impatiently dismissed the men as quickly as he had summoned them. He thought to himself, "Murder has always been a fact of life in Rome. Who can forget Julius Caesar's death during the Ides of March? Emperor Caligula only survived three years after Augustus' death before senators killed him. Even Emperor Claudius has thwarted his own assassination several times. He is still alive."

Maybe he could fabricate the murder of that teacher Jeshua that would somehow influence the masses. Jeshua had been extremely disliked by the Jewish leaders. However, the message he taught was being embraced by many who heard it. After all, the elders of the village had attempted to continue the sermons after Jeshua's death before they were removed from the village and brought to Rome. The Jewish judges and priests were losing control of their people. This had the potential to lead to trouble with Rome. Perhaps a revolt in Palestine could be fabricated. The Jewish people had certainly revolted many times in the past, especially during Passover. There had been a small riot this past year when one soldier had made a rude gesture. A few thousand Jews had had to be restrained. Many were killed in the upheaval. They did get riled up easily. What would be wrong with another revolt, even if it hadn't happened?

Noise from the street startled Brutus. Another festival, another celebration passing under his window. Would it ever stop, or at least be limited, he asked himself: "Which god are they trying to appease this time?"

Then he had an idea. Since some gods like the Greek God Zeus and the Hebrew God were feared, his new religion must produce fear. Fear like he produced in his court. Yes, he was a master at generating fear. "Why did I not think of this sooner?" Brutus mumbled to himself. "A large-scale fear of something throughout the Empire and Rome will be prosperous again," Brutus said out loud. "Yes! A religion that puts fear into the hearts of all. A religion based on domination over its subjects would generate fear. Such a religion would solve the problems of Rome. Rome would return to the glory that was her right. Her greatness would cause the world to tremble. All would fall to their knees in honor of her splendour.

"A religion that generates fear, pure raw fear!" Brutus yelled to the bare walls. His illumination was both riveting and startling. He paused to collect his breath. Speaking out loud again, Brutus reasoned, "To generate fear among citizens and subjects, there must be an overall creator of that fear. Yes, adopt a god that is like Zeus and the Hebrew God who is vengeful, both demanding to be worshipped and feared." However, Brutus had heard from his spies that the teachings of Jeshua stated his God was not like that, but was compassionate and caring. He thought to himself for a moment and concluded, "We can easily disprove that by saying Jeshua was murdered by his loving God. The myth should be something like that." Pondering that idea, he asked himself, "How could a fictitious murder be convincing?" Mentally resting on that question and not seeing an answer, his thoughts moved on.

The new religion would need some symbols to constantly remind the people of Rome and the Empire of this change. Perhaps the same figures that were being used in present worship, festivals and even past traditions. Images that were common in different cultures, emblems such as the cross, the circle and the number four. Perhaps the murder could be blamed on four bandits from the west bank of the Upper Nile. It would have to occur far away from Rome so no one could verify or disprove the event. Brutus pondered on the symbol of the cross. From Eastern Hindu mystics to Egyptian priests, all had used a cross-shaped symbol in their religious rituals. It was an indication of life and abundance. It also symbolized the pattern of the sun as it traveled around the earth. Ancient Babylon used the cross as a representation of their Sun God Shamash; others had used it to denote the four directions of the earth: north, east, south and west. Ancient Assyrian kings and some Greek goddesses had used the cross in their symbology. To astrologers, the cross could represent the four fixed signs of the zodiac. Yes, the cross, incorporated since early Greek times by many different traditions, would be included in the fantasy. The fictitious murder must involve a cross.

Then Brutus suddenly had his most brilliant idea. Since Jeshua had ignored the demands of the judges and Temple priests of his Hebrew tradition, he would be described as a brilliant but misguided teacher. His God did not love as he claimed, but was indeed vengeful to those who disobeyed him. His God would make arrangements for the Pharisees to invite the soldiers to Jerusalem when the teacher would be speaking. His words would be interpreted as offensive to the Emperor. The Emperor's Consul would deal with this crime swiftly and have Jeshua killed. The usual punishment for agitators was being nailed to a tree; he would be nailed to a cross. It would be asserted he was the son of an angry Hebrew God. All the subjects of the Empire would agree that a father who had allowed his son to be killed must be feared. A Father who watched his son being tortured would be rejected. A Father who would abandon his son could not be trusted. He must make this God be shunned by the subjects. The followers of Jeshua all felt their God was approachable and compassionate. These beliefs must be changed. Fear must dominate. Fear must overshadow everything. Brutus thought he could make this work. He was, after all, a master of creating fear.

Brutus was excited and exhausted at the same time. He needed a break. He went to the bath. There were no new attendants, no delicacies, no women in the side rooms, no favors to be had. He longed for those better times. He cursed. It was time to see the Emperor.

ROME
THE FORUM

"Self-determination, you are the leader of yourself; you can connect with the spirit that created the stars, the planets, the trees, the wind and the sun. You are a part of this Creation. It is in your heart. The Kingdom is within. You need no others to tell you how to live." Matthos remembered these words from Teacher's lessons. He was now far away from the village olive tree where Teacher had shared his knowledge with him. Some time had passed. Now he was hearing these words from a man who called himself a guru speaking to a small crowd near the Forum. How did these words leave Palestine? How did they get to Rome? Or was he in Rome? He seemed to be in a place with very high mountains, unlike anything he had seen in the Mediterranean.

Matthos woke briefly from his dreamy sleep; a strange feeling of longing overcame him. He was hungry; he fell back to his mystical vision. He seemed to fly like a huge seabird back to a softly lit mountain range. Orange and purple wild flowers dotted a gently sloping green alpine meadow. Many people were celebrating the rising of the morning sun. All were seated cross-legged with eyes closed, the way Teacher had greeted each morning. There was rejoicing for the discovery of personal power that came with a connection with Creation, with God. It appeared as if Teacher's lessons were finally being accepted as they were intended to be. No religious leaders were demanding false respect and worship. All were celebrating their Oneness. There were no wars, no fears and all were treated with respect. Everyone was free in Spirit. Compassion and empathy enveloped everyone. Teacher's truth evidently prevailed somewhere.

Matthos' vision projected to the winter solstice of 2063 A.D. There is a sudden massive earthquake that destroys a small part of Rome across the Tiber River from the Campus Martius, a district filled with darkness and deceit, a Rome he does not recognize. Large round stone and concrete rooftops crash to the ground disintegrating into pieces. Colonnades are reduced to rubble. Glass windows are shattered into fragments. Crosses of wood and metal are strewn about and distorted. Many men in black, white and red robes are crushed and killed by the collapsing buildings. Everything is reduced to a pile of rubble, the destruction all-encompassing. There seems to be a collective sigh of relief from the celestial heavens. Compassion envelopes the confused departed souls, for their crimes were great. Many Angels assemble to help the lost spirits annihilated by the destruction. Their hatred has consumed them. Their lusts have devoured them. The Angels guide them to rest beside a smooth flowing foggy river. The light is soft and dim. A boatman soon appears in a small open fishing boat. One by one they are transported through the mist. The other side of the river is obscured. From out of the fog, their soul-wrenching and long lingering cries pierce the air as they witness the lives they lived.

Matthos did not understand the meaning of his vision. It appeared a small country within a future Rome's boundary had been destroyed. The tiny country spread hatred, immorality and false truths in the name of a religion throughout the world. The Angels were helping the lost souls while at the same time rejoicing. It appeared as if Creation itself had seen enough and ordered the removal and destruction of this horrid organization.

~

Matthos was jolted awake by the cold hard boot of a soldier striking his ribs. He was ordered to leave the temple. The smell of Rome pierced his nostrils. He was very hungry. He followed the masses to the games at the Circus Maximus. Food was being distributed to all who asked. He heartily ate the tasty roasted pig and tart pickled fish. The cool beer was most refreshing. He ate in silent confusion. His dream was bizarre and mysterious. Yet somehow it was comforting and reassuring at the same time.

He was astounded at the hundreds of people milling about the Circus Maximus. They all were partaking of the food provided. As he knew no one in Rome, he decided to stay and watch the entertainment that would begin in a few hours.

~

Elsewhere in the city... The slaves from Village 42 working in Brutus' library buried beneath the streets of Rome were extremely surprised to discover journals written by Matthos. He had called one the Gospel of Jeshua. There was also a Gospel of Matthos which recorded the sermons Teacher had given under the olive trees and throughout Palestine. The Lessons talked about God as being fair, concerned and loving, not vengeful as the Pharisees claimed. They were written in the parables told by Jeshua, who had recognized the search for truth needed to be cloaked in symbolism.

The slaves discovered the poem of Meaning and Self-Realization that Jeshua had given to the people, beginning with "Our Father". That collection of poetic lines had meant so much to the villagers as they had experienced for themselves the transformation that occurred with steadfast application of the poem. They were saddened that the teachings of Jeshua's messages had ceased. Hopefully, others who had heard the Lessons would keep the stories alive. They hoped the Lessons would remain intact and not be misrepresented.

They recalled how Jeshua had talked about that man from India named Buddha. At his death, Buddha told all present not to view him as their leader or savior. Rather they should follow their own minds and souls using his words as guidelines, not rules. Then they would discover their own enlightenment. They would find the pathway of the ancient mystics as he had after many days of meditation. However, upon his death, some of his followers had distorted his teachings. The group split into two factions. Despite the differences, Jeshua had found that when he contemplated the main message from the Buddha, his own inner sun guided him to his personal Truth. He felt the Buddha would have been pleased. Jeshua had often wondered out loud whether the words of Moses had suffered the same fate as the teachings of his spiritual friend from India. He felt the real message given to his people by Creation through Moses was meant to be personal and not collective in nature. The slaves recalled how Jeshua had shared with them his own visions of the Angel. It had proved to him the sacredness of individual life. They all sat in silence remembering their friend and teacher.

Peterus could not get out of his mind that Matthos was in Rome. He shared this with Thomas. They developed a plan. During the games, the guards became very preoccupied with the entertainment and lost track of their charges. Matthos would be hungry; he would certainly find his way to the Circus Maximus.

ROME
EMPEROR'S PALACE

Emperor Claudius had observed Brutus. He avoided controversy. He was never involved in any assassination attempts, yet he seemed to be aware of everything. Perhaps a lifetime as a magistrate had trained his mind to perceive the inner thinking of men.

Whenever Emperor Claudius personally sat in the courts, he had often noticed Brutus not agreeing with him. His judgments were not always in accordance with Roman law. That didn't matter, he was the Emperor. When Claudius shortened the traditional court breaks and extended the summer and winter court sessions, Brutus had not been amused. Claudius didn't care, he was the Emperor. After he demanded plaintiffs and defendants stay in Rome until their cases were heard, he saw how the courts and Brutus operated more efficiently. Emperor Claudius was proud of the changes he had made to the Roman justice system.

Emperor Claudius was always concerned about his subjects. He followed in the footsteps of Augustus in attempting to get the cult of Caesar accepted and embraced by all. Placing statues of Emperor Augustus deified after his death in temples with gods like Apollo, Mars, Vesta and Neptune was giving more credibility to Emperor worship. However, something needed to be added. There were still too much sun worshipping and too many festivals for every god from every culture. This all detracted from Emperor worship and the needs of Rome. When the Emperor received the request from Brutus for an audience, he looked forward to meeting with him. He needed an update on the progress on Brutus' plans for restructuring festivals, the concept he had presented to the Congress.

When his attendants notified the Emperor that Brutus had arrived at the palace, he had him escorted to a private chamber. "Welcome, my friend. What new order have you devised for us, dear Brutus?" the Emperor asked.

Brutus replied, straight to the point, "The Cult of Caesar and Emperor worship is weakening. The Emperors are either assassinated or poisoned. They don't rule long enough for the subjects to embrace their leader, plus their untimely deaths raise questions regarding their divinity. Only Augustus ruled for forty years. All his successors have had short terms. If this continues, subjects will abandon the idea of Emperor superiority and continue worshipping their ancestors and various long-standing gods."

Brutus paused so Claudius could grasp what he was saying. After all, Claudius was very swift in dealing with his perceived enemies. Perhaps he was being too blunt but since he was still alive, he presented his proposal. "We will start a new public religion of Rome. It will be based on three testaments. Firstly, there will be one God who is outside of each and every mortal being. Secondly, only the graces of this God can change a person's lot and reduce or eliminate suffering. These graces can only be granted by a few appointed members of our Church. And thirdly, a subject can only receive these graces if he is a member of our new religion. Rome will be prosperous and the Imperial rule of yourself and all future Emperors will be protected."

Brutus paused again to gauge the reaction of Claudius. The Emperor's eyes were fixed on him. He continued,

"One God disconnected from man is not a new concept, as everyone knows the gods are celestial spirit entities and above all subjects. But too many gods confuse and distract the citizens. We will educate the masses to one God. Also, our God will have a mortal son, just as all mortal Roman rulers have fathers who are gods. He will be deified upon his death, just as all emperors are now. We will use the Jeshua Christus philosophy from Palestine. His teachings were not accepted by the local leaders but he had a dedicated following in the east. This antagonism will give us a large and immediate membership for our new religion. Of course, the teachings will be altered to create fear, not hope for spiritual liberty and personal freedom. All evidence of the original lessons will be destroyed. Since his death is recent, I am sure there are not many documents of his words."

Again, Brutus stopped to observe the reaction of the Emperor. He seemed interested so far. "This new religion of Rome will be celebrated at the same time of year as Saturnalia is now. This will ensure complete acceptance as all look forward to this oldest and most popular celebration each year. It will replace Saturnalia. The religion will be intolerant of others. No other customs will be tolerated, as is the case now by Roman rules. If they are not for our church we will consider them against us. All who do not convert to our new religion will be driven out of the Empire or executed in a painful public display. Fear must prevail. Nothing can distract the subjects from their duties to the new religion and the desires of Rome and her leaders. The church will set the date for all other festivals. There will be fewer so the subjects can attend to their tasks." Brutus paused again to get a glimpse of Claudius' reaction. He continued to appear interested.

Brutus resumed, "We will create a myth where the teacher Jeshua was sacrificed by his father God in order to show the error of his teachings. We will expose his father God as not compassionate but demanding of servitude, and to be feared. Our God will not be benevolent; he will be judgmental, punishing and vengeful towards all, even to his own son. Our God's son will be born under a magnificent star just as Augustus' rule of Rome was born under the Star of Caesar. He will be sacrificed by his cruel Father God on a cross, a widely used symbol in all cultures. This will also attract the sun-worshippers who use the symbol of a cross in their ceremonies. The Emperor will be supreme leader of this new Imperial religion. We will eventually conquer the entire world not using soldiers, but using a religion based on fear. Rome will dominate and prosper. The entire world will send its wealth to the new Roman church. Our way will be the envy of all rulers."

"Brutus, your ideas are very radical. Do you really think we can persuade all of Rome to abandon their rituals to their ancestors and their gods? Do you think we can convince the subjects that only one God exists? Even if we could, it would take some time. However, your plan is brilliant."

Claudius called his personal guards. "Imprison this man at once. Do not let him escape. Secure him tightly." He whispered to himself, "Only one person in Rome can know about this new religion—the Emperor!"

The first step in Brutus' proposal was to incite a Jewish uprising and steal their Torah. The altered writings of Jeshua Christus, who was born a Jew, would be added to the Torah. He had been controversial and had had a very large following in the Eastern provinces. They would find immediate refuge from the upheaval in a new religion of Rome that included their Torah and Jeshua's wisdom, albeit changed. This would attract new cult members quickly.

Since all recorded knowledge must reflect the dogma of the new church, every manuscript of Jeshua's original teachings must be destroyed. Claudius reasoned that some manuscripts containing ancient Egyptian and Greek philosophy had to disappear as well. As Rome had conquered all the surrounding lands of the Mediterranean, the soldiers could accomplish this task quickly. Truth must be vanquished from the Roman Empire for the new religion to grow. It must dominate, creating servitude and fear. All subjects must be forced to adhere to the new state religion.

Claudius felt the wildly popular Saturnalia festival should be maintained for social morale. It would be moved to March to correspond with the days and nights being equal. Spring was the time of year when crops were reborn from the cold winter by the warming sun, something that required commemorating annually. Possibly he could invent a religious resurrection celebration for the spring in this new religion. After all, Zeus resurrected Cybele's lover with the greening spring vegetation. A festival honoring the myths of the new church would replace the Saturnalia celebration times in Decembris. Daily household rituals seeking protection from the Lares and other deceased ancestors needed to be revised to suit the new cult church. The wine and bread ceremony could become a daily remembrance for their fictitious Son of God.

The Emperor sat in his chair and contemplated how to implement this plan. It would take some time. It may need revisions, but it would work. He would not see the complete scope of this new state religion during his reign, but future emperors would ultimately look back and acknowledge his contribution to their power and opulence. He would be gloriously deified many times in the future. What a wonderful, almost mystical innovation! Rome would be all powerful and protected from future invading armies. A religion is carried forward even if a culture is defeated using force. Claudius was consumed by thoughts of global control over all peoples of the earth. What an honor for Rome! She would prevail in either military success or failure. She would be the future for the human race. She would be the Truth. She would be divine. She would be the Jupiter for all to worship.

Claudius was jolted from his thoughts by the loud protests of Brutus as he was dragged away by the guards. Another enemy awaited his fate. Claudius held a tight ring of control over his advisors. A public execution for tomorrow's games was required. The spectators always demanded blood.

ROME
CIRCUS MAXIMUS

The hard stone floor at Circus Maximus was cold and uncomfortable. The cell was small and dark. The blood on his face was still damp. Brutus had lost consciousness when the soldiers threw him onto the unyielding floor. What had happened? What had he said that offended the Emperor? He drifted off to an unusual hallucination.

Fifteen years had passed; it was now 66 A.D. The Greeks and Hebrews in Judea had started another religious skirmish. This time it had escalated to a revolt against taxation and many Roman citizens in the area were killed. General Vespasian and his son Titus were eventually sent by Rome to put down the rebellion. With four legions of soldiers, the Jews in Judea were attacked and systematically defeated. During this campaign, in 68 A.D. Emperor Nero committed suicide and after three failures in a year, the senate declared Vespasian the new Emperor of Rome. He returned to his new duties, via Egypt, and his son Titus completed the campaign against the Jews. He entered Jerusalem in 7o A.D. The Temple was looted and destroyed. The city was completely razed and left in ruins. Their Torah was stolen and the survivors transported to Rome. They were enslaved to build the new Flavian Amphitheater. It was completely round and enclosed—a gift to the Roman citizens from the new Emperor Vespasian. Within its walls, crowds of people (up to eighty thousand) enjoyed gladiator fights and public executions, entertainment similar to the Circus Maximus. Even military victories were re-enacted so the people could witness the power of Rome. Such demonstrations also showed the subjects the folly of trying to rebel against the might of the authorities. Food was served during these spectacles, everything was free.

In 115 A.D. the Jews and Greeks started fighting again, this time in Alexandria, Egypt. The Jews were dispatched away from the Eastern Mediterranean completely. However, their Torah remained in Rome stored in the hidden library under the Justice Hall. It had been placed with all the other confiscated Palestinian books including the writings from Village 42, the Gospels of Maria, Matthos, Peterus, Thomas, Marcus, and the Gospel of Truth and the Gospel of Peace. They remained undisturbed for almost three hundred years.

In his hallucination, Brutus saw that the Cult of Caesar was not successful and did not gain the acceptance the senators and emperors had anticipated. They finally decided that Rome needed a vastly different religion, a new state religion that controlled the subjects' activities through domination and fear, exactly as Brutus had imagined. However, the priests and higher priests, called bishops, were not in agreement with the laws and rituals of the new church. There was much confusion, dissention and many contradictions within the churches throughout the Empire.

Brutus' dream advanced to 325 A.D. at the Council of Nicaea in the Eastern province. In an attempt to get the church properly organized and preaching the same message to all citizens, Emperor Constantine summoned all the bishops in the Empire (about eighteen hundred) and some of their priests to a gathering at his summer palace. The Council was charged with settling the disputes between regions of the Empire regarding the nature of God and his son. Emperor Constantine opened the sealed library under the Justice Hall in Rome and found the Jewish Torah and the writings of Jeshua. He assumed they were meant to be together. They would be part of the discussion at Nicaea. Surrounded by the opulence of the central Imperial Palace, Brutus could hear their deliberations.

"If we are to use this teacher Jeshua's material for our church, we must scrutinize it closely. There are too many collections written by Matthos, Marcus, Lucas, Phillip, Thomas, Maria and Johnus. There are essays called Gospels of Truth, Gospels of Peace, and Gospels of the Teacher. There are thirteen collections. This must be reduced drastically." The speaker paused for a moment then continued. "We will select only four, as the sun divides the passage of its travel through the heavens into four seasons. The number four represents the completion of a cycle of existence, as well as the directions of the earth. It is a common number among many cultures. We must use familiar symbols for mass appeal."

Brutus could hear a reading from the Gospel of Thomas and the Gospel of the Teacher, everyone listening closely. He could hear clearly, as if he were there himself, "If one does not understand how the fire came to be, he will burn in it, as he does not know his root. If one does not first understand the water, he does not know anything. If one does not understand how the wind that blows comes to be, he will run with it. If one does not understand how the body that he wears came to be, he will perish with it. Whoever does not understand how he came will not understand how he will go."

The speaker expressed his opinion. "This man was encouraging people to think for themselves, to make discoveries about their personal nature and to abandon customary rituals. He encouraged contemplation upon the natural physical world. How can one understand any more about the ways of fire and wind? We use wind to sail our boats and fire to heat our villas, prepare our food and make offerings to the gods. The people do not need to know more than this. There is nothing more to understand."

The reading continued, "I have often been asked; what is the place to which we shall go? My answer is to the place which you can reach and stand. There is light within a man of light and it lights up the whole world. If he does not shine he is darkness. Go within. As to someone's ignorance, when he comes of knowledge, his ignorance vanishes by itself; as darkness vanishes when light appears, so also the deficiency vanishes in the fulfillment."

The speaker pondered aloud, "Such words of encouragement to spend time to understand yourself are the ramblings of a lunatic. However, many have listened to these words and embraced them. This man was a teacher in Palestine for twenty years."

He returned to the writings. "The kingdom is inside of you. When you come to know yourselves, then you will be known, and you will realize that you are the sons of the Living Father. But if you will not know yourselves, then you dwell in poverty, and it is you who are that poverty. Our priests tell us this kingdom is in the sky, if that is true then the birds will arrive before you. If they say to you the kingdom is in the sea, then the fish will arrive before you. Rather, the kingdom is a state of self-discovery, the discovery of your inner sun. The kingdom is within you."

The speaker paused and read ahead silently to himself. Then he gasped and read aloud, "You may compare me to other people. You may think I am a wise philosopher, you may see me as a righteous Angel. But I am not your master. If this is what you believe, you have become drunk as from drinking too much wine. You have become drunk on what I have been saying. You must navigate the road to the Kingdom within on your own."

A bishop from Britannia jumped to his feet. "This man was insane! No leader asks his men for their opinion. All leaders tell their subjects what to do, what to think and where to go. Can you think of any successful warrior general who did not tell his soldiers what to do? From Alexander the Great to Julius Caesar and Augustus, the leaders of men told their fighters what to believe and how to act. Imagine our generals trying to do battle with over four thousand soldiers, archers and mounted fighters, all which make up just one Roman legion, and not give direction during the battle. Some battles involve seven legions on either side, thousands of soldiers. If all these fighters were following their inner sun for direction in battle there would be no victories … ever!

"If we are to use the teachings of this man, we must invent some powerful leadership. He must be seen as a mighty dominant son of God as well as a mortal. All leaders have these qualities. He must be heard giving orders. His way is the only way, just as our victors in battle make all the decisions and send the troops to glory. It is their brilliance that brings about victories. Soldiers take orders from their leaders." The bishop sat down as quickly as he had stood up.

Another priest stood and exclaimed, "These words must be destroyed. If we are to restructure the daily activities of subjects for the benefit of our church, they must have no motivation for self-discovery. They must take directions from the leaders of the new religion."

The reading continued. "You must discover your own mind. It is the father of your truth. You need to know yourself in silence. The teachings of the East direct one to sit in meditative silence. You must develop your own independent authority and not submit to anyone else's authority."

Brutus could see all the bishops and priests squirm in their seats as they heard these words. A gasp went through the great hall.

"When you see the spirit you will become the spirit, you will see yourself and what you see, you shall become."

The speaker put the codices down and in frustration exclaimed, "These words must be changed, or destroyed. Our church cannot function when the teachings tell subjects to search within themselves. This man has developed a large and faithful following since his death. However, there is still time to alter the words to suit our purpose. We must have the efforts of our citizens focused on the needs of Rome, her leaders and the Emperor.

"People are not beings of light. They are subjects of the Roman Emperor. We must maintain the Roman and Greek philosophy that the gods are separate from men. Since this man was Jewish, we must also adopt the same Jewish teachings that men and God are completely separate. We must change these Gospels."

It was put forward … "The Gospels of Matthos, Lucus, Marcus and Johnus seem to be similar. We will use them. The remainder, especially this Gospel of Thomas, will be destroyed. We will begin with revising the Gospel of Johnus. When people ask of Jeshua, 'We do not know where you are going, how can we know the way?' we will insert what any powerful divine leader would say—I am the way, the truth and the life. No one comes to the truth but by me.' We will put these words in the mouth of Jeshua. All will believe them to be true.

"Then our hero Jeshua must be fully deified as the Son of God. He will be born of a virgin mother impregnated by a divine being, just as the ancient Egyptian queen. A noble star will appear at his birth, like the Star of Caesar. His deification will prove him to be a Son of God. Since the Jewish people have been waiting for a messiah, we will make Jeshua their Messiah. He will be sacrificed as in the old customs. We must devise a story that is so absurd that it will be believable. Symbols and daily rituals must be established to enhance our grip over the masses."

There was a muted silence among the gathering as the bishops contrived a myth. Finally Emperor Constantine spoke. "As the sun rises every morning after its death the previous evening, and as Cybele provides resurrection to those who appease her, we will have Jeshua actually appear in the flesh after his death. After all, he did make himself known in spirit to his close friends following his passing. We will make changes to the Gospels and have him demand of these followers to touch his resurrected physical body. This is so absurd that the uneducated will believe it, especially since he will be portrayed as the Son of God. As the Son of God, he will have miraculous powers of resurrection of physical life, just as the sun brings life back to the cold earth every spring. We will humanize him, giving him all the Natural powers of the Sun God. We will create stories of his powers to raise the dead, just as stories were generated from Egypt that Emperor Vespasian had healing powers. Jeshua will be their Messiah and savior from all suffering here on earth and the afterlife. He will be our pawn. We will use him to attract a congregation to our church. We will prosper beyond our imagination.

"Also, one can only secure the blessings of Jeshua through our church. Outside the church there is no hope, faith, or favor from the gods, or rather from the one God. This will ensure that the subjects of Rome will adhere to the dogma of our religion. He will be their Messiah. He will die for them. They need not seek their personal comfort from the gods. They need not offer gifts to their deceased ancestors. They need not worship the sun. Everything has been done for them by this Messiah, Son of God. They can now concentrate on the needs of Rome, the Emperor and its new church."

All the bishops murmured in agreement. One rose and spoke. "We need a simple symbol for our church, something that will constantly remind subjects of our new religion. We need a symbol for this son, the offspring of God. Our astrologers use the symbol of the ram for the spring cycle of the natural sun. Since the offspring of a ram is a lamb, we will adopt the image of a lamb with brilliant warm and resurrecting rays of the spring sun emanating from its body. This will be our symbol for the divine Son of God." The bishops adopted the changes. The myth of the Lamb of God would begin immediately.

~

In his dream, Brutus suddenly experienced a flash of brilliant light where the lamb was replaced three hundred years later by a grotesque image of a murdered man. He was hanging, nailed at his hands and feet to the sacred symbol of the sun-worshippers, a cross. This image appeared everywhere.

~

Back in Nicaea, Brutus heard the Council members' discussion. The meeting places for the new church would be the many basilicas built throughout the Roman territories. The halls were very large and subjects would accept truth and judgement coming from these buildings. An altar would be placed at the end that was rounded. If both ends were rounded, only one altar would be built.

The bishops voted unanimously to create only one God who created all the heavens and earth. References to all ancient gods from Roman and Greek existence were removed. Manuscripts were destroyed. The single God was similar to the Hebrew God, a God of judgment, vengeance and fear. The official myth of Jeshua as a Son of that God was established. In an attempt to attract ordinary Romans to the new cult, his name was changed to be more Roman. It became Jessus Christus. The Torah remained intact and was referred to as "The Old", but the writings concerning the teachings of Jeshua were edited drastically. Any references to self-liberating ideas were removed and the necessary dictatorial ways of Divine Roman leadership were inserted. It was called "The New". The new state religion was based on fear and domination. Subjects had no hope beyond prescribed dictates from the church. Any scriptures and books of truths held by unofficial persons were confiscated and either burned in public or stored with other volumes under the Justice Hall in Rome. The Justice Hall would be the headquarters for the new state religion.

Jessus was portrayed as a Son of God, just like all the great leaders since Augustus. He died at the hands of a Roman court like all other antagonistic revolutionaries, his hands and feet nailed to a tree trunk and its lowest limbs, in a cross pattern, and left to die, just like all rebels against Rome. This diminished the effect of his writings and contradicted his teachings. His message had been that God was compassionate. His death showed the opposite. His God would not save him.

The daily lararium rituals were dedicated to this new Son of God. The bread and wine symbolized his body and blood, just as Brutus had always enjoyed after his victims. Eventually, the lararium was declared unholy and all worship moved to the basilicas to be directed by a greater person, a priest. Small altars were allowed to replace the lararium, but little power was associated with these local places of worship.

The odor of animals pierces Brutus' nostrils as he wakes up on the stone floor of the holding area of the Circus Maximus. He cannot understand the fantasy he has witnessed. His plan seems to have been somehow activated. He is seeing it implemented throughout the Empire. He can now feel the heat of a huge fire. He returns to his apparition, now in a different time.

In 391 A.D. the library at the Museum in Alexandria Egypt was destroyed by fire. Soldiers of the new church could be seen destroying non-flammable statues and symbols of Truth. Over seven hundred thousand books and tablets were destroyed. The wax tablets burned quickly and contributed to the rapid and complete destruction of this reservoir of knowledge. Collections of mankind's studies and observations of himself and his environment were destroyed, as Brutus had envisioned. However, the continuing destruction of books after this event brought much criticism from the populace. Therefore, books were then shipped to Rome and stored with other material stolen from other cultures and traditions. The Truths had to be quashed. They could not be allowed to circulate among the masses. Other writings were found, confiscated and hidden under the Justice Hall. Much truth was buried there.

In order to attract subjects to the new religion, the promise of food and proper burial was given. The social situation was so unstable that unrest and outright revolts were breaking out constantly, both in Rome and throughout the Empire. People were hungry. Families were being killed. The church would offer proper burial for the dead, a single burial place with a small stone to mark the grave. All open burial pits around Rome were filled with sand and never used again.

The new state religion initially attracted slaves, women and some lower class Romans. It was perceived as helpful in maintaining the social structure. It helped maintain the upper echelons of Roman rule by calming the unrest. The baths could be enjoyed without fear of invading hordes of hungry people. The Senate could go on with its work and luxuries.

Saturnalia was replaced with a festival honoring the deceit of the church, and the make-believe birth of Jessus Christus. The new date was moved from Decembris 17 to Decembris 25, to coincide with the day the Sun moved into the longer days of light. Sun worship was still very popular in the Empire despite attempts to stop the practice. This date was incorporated into the new church's rituals to broaden its appeal beyond the followers of Jeshua and to include the many Sun-worshippers.

The concept of a single God separate from man was emphasized, a God that passed judgments and was feared and also vindictive. This was the only way the leaders of the new religion could continue to ensure the prosperity of Rome. She had to continue in her barbaric ways. She must dominate the entire world.

Brutus is suddenly awakened by the hard damp boot of a guard striking his ribs. The uneven stones of the floor are digging into his flesh. The blood has dried on his face. He has a raging headache. He wonders where his illusion is coming from. He quickly falls back to sleep. The strange story continues.

The Empire was gone. Rome had fallen. The soldiers had vanished. The Emperor had disappeared. There was an old bishop called the Pope. A new church existed, designed after the Roman army. Generals were now called priests. Marriage of priests was forbidden as it had been for the legion soldiers. Absolute authority was with the Pope, just as the cult of Caesar had given absolute authority to the Emperor. The church suppressed truth, created fear, demanded servitude and dominated its subjects.

All the Greek schools of thought throughout the Empire were closed by decree of the Pope. Their materials were scattered and destroyed. Some had found their way to the vault of hidden truths beneath the Justice Hall. Knowledge from the astrologers and magicians had also been stolen and destroyed or hidden.

Much land had been confiscated to make room for the promise of proper burial. Just as the Roman armies confiscated land in the conquered countries to build Roman towns, the new church was following the practices of the legions and their generals. Huge cathedrals to honor this state religion were built to replace the basilicas. This activity enslaved carpenters, stonemasons, craftsmen and their children for several generations. During this construction the rules of the church were embedded into the masses over these generations thus destroying any hope of personal salvation other than through their son of God, Jessus. His graces were only available through the designated generals of the church, the priests.

Everything was structured just as Brutus had suggested to the Emperor. Priests were given the luxuries of the Roman baths and access to young boys and girls for their pleasures. The priesthood had grown into a secret cult of sexual abuse, particularly of young boys. Millions of pounds of gold were spent in hiding this activity. Offerings that were given by the congregations to help the church were being diverted to the priests for their sinister pleasures. Food, delicacies and imported wine and beers were always available for the priests, even as members of the church were starving. Wives were forbidden. Too many riches had been inherited by wives and children in the early days when priests were allowed to marry. Their wealth had been passed on to their families. The church stopped this outflow of wealth and hoarded the abundance it demanded from its subjects. Families were strained by the dictates of the Pope. He demanded the birth of many children to expand his religion. Families resided around the cathedrals, worked the fields for food, tended the animals and built the structures. They also provided the necessary helpers and pleasures for the priests, whatever or whoever was required.

Brutus saw the rise of the understanding of Nature and the physical laws it followed—Science. The earth was not flat, but round. The earth revolved around the sun. This new knowledge threatened the ways of the Church. Everyone knew the earth was the center of Creation. If science was studied and understood, people would start to realize their self-reliance. The position of the Church would be undermined and weakened. Therefore, courts or Inquisitions were set up to punish any who entertained ideas not in accordance with the dogma of the church. Science was declared heresy by the Pope. Scientists such as Galileo were banned from the church and placed under house arrest. Soon those who were considered heretics were burned alive. Anything to create fear among the general masses was used. Absolute authority had to prevail. All subjects were kept ignorant of Truths and in servitude and fear.

The Church of Rome was a resounding success; all popes were considered the Supreme Being in the flesh, just as the Emperors of the Roman Empire had been. The myth of Jessus was being embraced by many and the congregations were dedicating themselves to the needs of the Church and its leaders.

The Roman habit of Empire building by conquering others continued. Now, however, no respect was given to the customs of the conquered. Other cultures were annihilated. Crusades of horsemen slaughtered those who did not join the Cult. Just as revolts against the Roman state had been suppressed, barbaric public tortures were used to keep subjects in line.

Priests followed the adventurers who explored this newly discovered round planet. They destroyed indigenous beliefs and replaced them with the distortions of Jeshua's teachings. Families were torn apart and children were forbidden to speak their own language. They were abused emotionally and physically by the priests, anything to create fear and rob people of their dignity. All other religions and traditional customs of worship were damned.

The cult of Caesar had finally blossomed as it was envisioned by Augustus and Brutus. All forms of non-sanctioned sacredness were destroyed. The people became slaves of the Church. They provided food, pleasures and delicacies for the rulers, just like the Rome he knew as a young man. His plan was a resounding success. A small city within an expanded Rome grew to house the wealth and papal staff. The confiscated books of truth were transferred there from the Justice Hall. Massive colonnades, works of art and doomed roofs comprised the grounds. Many priests were ordained into the cult there and sent out into the world to plunder and destroy. The Church promoted itself as the protector of God himself on the face of the earth. It was awash in tremendous physical wealth. Much gold and silver was deposited along with the now massive library of hidden Truths in the bowels of the building that comprised the center of the new church's existence.

Brutus saw the Jewish community rise again as a race. He saw how the Church and the Pope joined with the Germanic tribes, who once defeated the Roman armies, to try and destroy the Jewish race again. Many were burned alive in large ovens overseen by the priests, in keeping with church law and tradition of dealing with heretics. The barbarianism, torture and bloodshed were ongoing.

Brutus saw in his hallucination the organization that he had envisioned, a religion with one God who only granted graces through its appointed priests. Graces were bestowed only to members of the church. Individuals were forced into servitude through fear and domination. Fear was generated by distortion and lies. Subjects were submitted to the myth that a son of God had died for them. They were constantly reminded of this falsehood with the wine and bread ritual. It was not tolerated to contact their mystical self, they had to remain a slave to the new church. They provided all the needs of the church. The church offered nothing in return but the deceitful promise of entry into the celestial heavens. If they followed the dictates of the Pope, the heavens would be theirs. If they did not, the damnation of living with the ancestors in the earth awaited them. Domination and fear gripped the entire congregation. The joy of life was quashed out of the subjects. Yes, Roman rule had prevailed and taken over the minds and souls of the masses. It had spread like a horrendous disease around this beautiful round orb called earth.

~

Brutus awakes to a partial awareness. He is extremely pleased. In his vision his plan has been realized. His mission to save Rome and restore her splendor has been accomplished. The Emperor Pope is protected and the pleasures of Rome have been restored. Brutus feels disoriented. He cannot distinguish whether this is real or a fantasy. A strong desire overtakes him. He wishes to enter the bath and enjoy the splendor of the attendants. Then he shudders on the cold stone floor of the Circus Maximus, the hard stones digging into his back. The desire vanishes. His curiosity is now aroused. If his dream was real, what is the name of this new Roman establishment? It is indeed a superb organization of domination and fear. It is beyond his imagination. He falls back to a partial sleep. He hears the answer to his question in a booming voice, a celestial voice like his own reverberating off the marble floors of his court in the Basilica Julia. The voice seems to encircle him completely. He hears the name. It is called the Universal Church of Rome, the Catholic Church of Rome.

A bucket of cold water thrown on Brutus jolts him awake. He cannot understand what his trance means. However, he is pleased with what he has seen. He is proud of his ideas. His fantasy confirms his proposal to be a complete solution. Through his stinging eyes, blurred from the cold water, he sees the Imperial guards surrounding him.

They abruptly and forcefully hoist him to his feet by his arms. Two sentries drag him into the Circus Maximus. His hallucinations still vivid in his mind, he is momentarily oblivious to his surroundings. He smiles as he recalls how his scheme appears to have succeeded in some mystical way. Then he becomes aware of the roar of the crowd in the stadium. The Emperor is standing in his marble enclosure and laughing. He gestures towards Brutus, then to the entire crowd and again towards the prisoner. Brutus realizes he is the extraordinary public execution for today. He reluctantly accepts his fate as he is tied to a post near the starting point for the chariot races. He stands proudly within the bounds of the stake. Brutus assumes the gods must be awaiting his entry into their heavens. He wishes the guards well as they leave the inner field. They cast a confused look back at the prisoner.

The wild beasts are pacing in their cages, eyes fixated on the prey tied to the post. The gates are raised and the lions are released. The starving creatures run at full speed towards the bound victim. The crowd erupts in a roar of approval. The anticipation of blood flowing excites everyone. The Emperor stands and raises his arms into the air in a show of victory. A beast leaps into the air towards the head of the bound chief magistrate. Just as the large jaws are about to clamp down on his neck, he screams out,

"I AM YOUR FIRST POPE!"

No one hears the words. His arm is severed at the shoulder. Blood spurts out from his upper body and stains the sand bright red. The claws of a roaring lion rip apart the flesh of his chest. His leg is crushed by the jaws of two other lions. His head rolls onto the bloody inner field. The roar of approval for the Emperor is deafening. The beasts devour the body parts. In just a few moments the only signs left of Brutus are a few bones and the bloody rags that were his clothes. The stake stands bared. The entertainment is exquisite and complete. The public execution by mauling of the beasts is the grand finale of the games.

The display over, the entire audience exits the stadium. They pass by the shrine to Cybele. Some pause briefly. Their lararia wait at their homes. The gods have to be appeased. So it is. Birds fly overhead. The evening air is cool and refreshing. The sun sets in the orange western sky. An illustrious full moon rises on the horizon.

A slow unholy darkness hovers over the stadium. A new Roman religion has been conceived. A horrible deception begins its descent and iron grip upon the masses. The Angels weep in the heavens. More than two thousand years are about to be lost. The darkness and deceit begin.

Peterus was right; he and Thomas find Matthos in the crowd. They quickly approach him and embrace for just a moment. Glancing back at the distracted guards, they swiftly leave for the docks by the river. The other slaves have a plan to disperse and travel to Galilee, each on his own. Matthos, Thomas and Peterus creep aboard a tow boat and hide among the bales. Their destination is the Museum at Alexandria. Rome is already a forgotten memory.

ROME
THE EMPEROR'S PALACE

Claudius is consumed with pride. His actions at the games have shown all of Rome his power. The mauling of Chief Magistrate Lupus Antonius Brutus was the highlight of public executions this year. Now he must focus on the beginnings of his church. The new Roman religion must be embraced by all. He ponders upon the irony that yet another Brutus has contributed to the evolution of Rome.

Palestine has always been trouble. Brutus was right about that. They resist paying the proper taxes. They rise up at the smallest provocation. Yes, a revolt must be arranged, but quietly. No one must suspect the source of the unrest. A special legion of soldiers will be assembled to create this new beginning.

The glory of Rome depends on this new revolution. The emperors of now and the future will be enshrined in their divinity. All will be prosperous and prevail. Claudius trembles with anticipation. He hopes he will live to see some of the splendor of this new church.

But it is not to be. Traitors find a way to remove him from the palace. He is quietly poisoned and replaced by Nero. Nevertheless his secret legion continues the work, loyal to the cause of Rome, regardless of who is emperor. Their legacy will prevail in the darkness and deceit.

UPPER EGYPT NEAR NAG HAMMADI 1945 A.D.

It is a bright day; the sun is warm and soothing. The Nile River flows peacefully toward the sea. Just before the big bend in the river, two peasants are going about their daily activity. They are digging for fertilizer at the base of the Jabal al-Tarif cliff. Just as they finish their tasks for the day, a shovel hits something solid. They clear away the sand and discover a buried earthen jar sealed at the mouth with a bowl. Thinking it may contain gold, they break it open. Inside are thirteen leather-bound codices, evidently extremely old. They carry them back to their village. The Lessons have been released from their two-thousand-year slumber.

Teacher is pleased. The Angels rejoice. The Truth will now be heard. Mankind will discover his individual inner Sun. Falsehoods will be destroyed. All will be united.

ACKNOWLEDGMENTS

The following publications were used as research for this book

Pagels, Elaine *The Gnostic Gospels*
New York: Random House 1979

Fox, Emmet *The Ten Commandments*
New York: Harper and Row 1953

Fox, Emmet *The Sermon on the Mount*
New York: Harper and Row 1938

Hall, Manly P *The Secret Teachings of All Ages*
New York: Various 1928

http://www.ancient.eu/index/

Plus too many websites to mention.

www.ingramcontent.com/pod-product-compliance
Lightning Source LLC
Chambersburg PA
CBHW02195?190626
46808CB00017B/2045